A FIGHT FOR HOME

REBUILDING HOPE
BOOK 2

P A WILSON

Ebook ISBN: 978-1-927669-44-0
Print book ISBN: 978-1-927669-43-3
Audio book ISBN:978-1-927669-58-7

FREE EBOOK

Claim your copy of A Choice to Make when you sign up for my newsletter and get a glimpse of Lena and Brian at the end of the plagues.

CHAPTER ONE

It was getting harder and harder to hide the fact that the ingredients she was using to make their meals were coming from outside the shelter. Pallavi stirred the pot of boiling water and added the chopped carrots and potatoes. At least she didn't have to explain the water; her father had gone to great lengths to ensure that they had access to fresh water from rainfall that was filtered to purity.

She glanced over her shoulder to see her brother, Mahir, chatting with her father. At nine years old he should be getting into trouble on the streets, not talking to their father about the best way to protect everyone if someone should breach the shelter defenses. Mahir was small for his age, and she couldn't help thinking that was because he hadn't been allowed to run in the sun for years. He'd been so young when their mother died. Pallavi was eleven when they first came to the shelter. She knew what it was like to feel the sun on her face. And now that she was sneaking out, she at least had some freedom.

"Daughter, the food is starting to smell delicious." Her father's voice was weak. He tried to hide it, but Pallavi knew he was ill. The next time she went out she must find some medicine.

Mahir walked over and took the spoon from her so she could continue preparing ingredients while he stirred.

"He will guess soon," Mahir whispered.

Pallavi ignored him. If her father became suspicious about how fresh the food was, she would think of a lie.

"Our garden has produced more than I could've hoped," her father said. Sometimes he seemed to read her mind. "You children have learned to garden well."

Pallavi had been hoping that the discussion would not come up for months. "It is like Mama is watching and helping us."

Her father liked to think his dead wife was watching over them. It was another sign of his illness, that he simply nodded and didn't launch into a long story about how her mother had been the best wife, the most loving mother.

Pallavi remembered her mother, and every time she looked in the mirror the reflection looked more like the woman her mother had been.

It was easier to keep her dark hair long because the shelter was supposed be sealed. That meant there was nowhere to dispose of clippings. At least as far as her father knew. He was so afraid of what might be going on outside their doors that he seemed to choose to believe they were more self-sufficient than they really were. She had her mother's gray eyes, and it looked like she was going to be the same height, although five and half feet could hardly be called height. The rest of her features she'd inherited from her father, her strong nose, her cheekbones, and her brown skin. And one more thing. Distrust of strangers.

The decision to go outside the first time took so long because Pallavi was convinced the world was full of danger. Only dire need had made her squeeze through the broken slats one night. Nothing bad had happened, but every time she ventured out, her stomach tightened, and her breath caught as she slid the loose wood aside.

"It has been a long time, Papa. Eventually we will have to go outside. When will we know it's safe?"

Her father coughed. It started as though he was clearing his throat, but then developed into a wheezing, compulsive gasp. Talking about going outside upset him, but never this much. She left Mahir at the fire and went to her father's side.

"It's okay, Papa. I'm sure it's not time yet. As you say, we still have a lot of vegetables." She handed him a glass of water and rubbed his back until the coughing subsided.

Ava moved the lantern to the end of the next row of shelves. When they'd found this root cellar, there had been no doubt it was where they would hide all their supplies. Three days of clearing and digging out some fallen areas gave them enough room to store all the harvest, preserves, and their dwindling supply of medicines.

It was a bonus that it was far enough away from the house that if they needed to, they could extend it without worrying about the foundations. And they could use the basement for storing things that needed to be kept dry, at least for now. She hoped, that eventually they would need the space for more bedrooms as more people joined them.

She looked at the next page in the notebook she used to keep track of what was left, so they knew what would happen as they got through winter.

"Four full barrels of carrots, unopened." She looked through the lattice they used to cap the barrels of vegetables and made a note. "I'll have to talk to Mellow," she muttered. "That's not what I call full."

The harvest had been good, but it was going to be tight over winter. With so few people to work the farm, they'd had to limit how much they planted. But if Lena's plan to create alliances worked out, maybe they would end up with some temporary workers from other communities so that they could supply food for the farm and a lot of other people.

She moved on to the next item on the list. *Cabbage, six crates. All full.* At least, that was what Mellow had written in the book. Ava didn't want to open the crates, but the one in front had too much space between the heads. The top was still in place, but if she was going to talk to Mellow about being precise, she needed to do it herself. Placing the book on the shelf, she hefted the crate onto the floor, and then jumped aside as three cabbages fell out.

"Dammit."

There was a missing slat in the back.

"Ava. We need you at the house."

Ava looked up to see Tik outlined in the doorway. His frame had filled out with the hard work on the farm, and he lost that slight edginess of a former gang banger.

"I need to finish in here," she said, grunting as she placed the crate back on the shelf. "And I need a new crate. Can you get it for me?"

Tik stepped through the doorway and walked to join her. He looked into the crate and whistled. "How many missing? Is it gonna be a problem?"

"I have to check all of them to see how many we need to replace. I don't think it's going to be a problem unless a lot of the crates are broken. And the cabbages that fell out might be somewhere under the shelving ready to be put back."

Tik pushed the crate a little further back on the shelf. "I'll help you do it later, but you need to come to the house now. We have a visitor. Lena wants all of us there when we talk to him."

"Someone from Crystal? They've come to tell us their decision on the alliance?" She picked up the lantern and stuck the notebook in her pocket.

"No, we're still waiting to hear from Crystal. I guess their council must hash everything out before they make a decision. This is someone we've met before. Come on."

Ava entered the back door of the farmhouse. She lay her notebook on the kitchen counter as she passed through. There were voices in the front of the house, so she assumed that was where she was needed. As she passed through the dining and living rooms, she hoped that it wasn't some kind of accident that needed medical supplies. Every time they used up some of the supply, it was just a little step closer to relying on folk remedies and herbal concoctions.

The front door was open, and Ava could see Keith and Deb standing just in front of the opening, both holding rifles. Just in front of them Lena stood blocking the stairs. So, not an accident.

She stepped between Keith and Deb, to see her son, Jason, also holding a gun. No matter how often she saw him go armed, it bothered her that such a young child would have to learn how to defend his home. He should be dealing with getting his first girlfriend at age thirteen, not facing down threats. That was the world now, the plagues had wiped out a way of living as well as so many of the children.

"Why should we trust you?" Lena asked. "The last time we saw you, we almost lost our freedom. And we did lose half of our supplies. You realize that almost killed us all."

Ava stepped up beside Lena as she spoke and saw who was standing on the path. Evan. That's the only name she had for him. On their journey to the farm, he'd been a guard at the Community of Truth, and complicit in his leader's plan to trap people and work them to death. Ava was surprised that Lena hadn't simply shot him, but then they would have to dispose of the body.

Ava watched as Evan held his arms out to the side, showing that he had no weapons within easy reach.

"Things have changed. Abigail is gone." He kept his arms out to his side, relaxed.

Ava turned to Lena and noticed Scott standing at the other end of the porch. "Did you check to see if he has any weapons hidden?"

Lena kept her eyes on Evan as she gestured to Scott. "I wasn't sure we would let him get this close. I'm still not sure we want to listen to him. But that's a good idea. Scott, pat him down."

They all watched carefully as Scott searched Evan. It didn't make sense that he wouldn't have some weapon.

"Where is everyone else?" Ava didn't want to take her attention away from Evan. Even though she didn't have a weapon, she wanted to make sure that there were no signs of a threat.

"You mean where are the kids?"

Lena knew her too well for Ava to deny it. "I could only see Jason. Where's Maya? And where's Mellow?"

"Maya is in her room. I suspect she's watching out of her window. Mellow went to the graves this morning."

When they had arrived at the farm almost a year ago, there were two people living there. Husband and wife, both too old to make the best of the farm. It had taken some effort, but Lena had convinced them that they were better off taking in the ragged group of people who had arrived at their door in a wagon, than letting the farm go to ruin. Over the winter both had succumbed to the flu.

"There's nothing," Scott called to the group on the porch. He stepped away from Evan and joined Lena, taking his rifle from where it leaned against the porch rail.

Ava wasn't convinced. Just because he didn't have anything on him didn't mean that Evan wasn't the bait in a trap. "You didn't come all this way without some kind of protection. Where is it? And did you walk?"

Evan lowered his arms, apparently thinking that he passed the test. "I left my weapons with my horse just down the road. I have a rifle, some ammunition, a bow and two quivers of arrows."

Ava could see that Lena wasn't sure what to do. Their history with this man and his community was enough to send him away. But they were so few, they needed alliances. That's why they had approached Crystal, a town a couple of days away, to make alliances, and make them both stronger.

Ava stepped a little closer to Lena to speak quietly. "It's going to be hard to learn what we need if he's standing that far away."

Lena uncrossed her arms, and beckoned Evan. "You're not entering the house. We'll do this on the porch. And anyone who wants to stay can stay."

As Evan walked up to join them, Ava tried to get Jason to leave, but he refused to budge. Scott said he would make some tea and disappeared into the house. Deb drifted away, but Keith stood his ground.

Ava went into the dining room and brought back two chairs. They might as well all be comfortable while they listened to what Evan had to say. Maya ran down the stairs and helped her by bringing another chair.

When they were settled, which meant that Ava and Lena sat at the small table placing Evan across from them leaving him no room to escape, the others shifted their weight, keeping their weapons ready.

"What do you mean Abigail is gone?" Lena asked. "She had a sweet deal there, in the Community of Truth, and no one seemed willing to make any changes when we came through."

Evan looked around, and then relaxed back in his chair. "Like I said, she's gone. Do you mind putting the guns down? I'd hate to have someone shot by accident."

Ava let Lena take the lead. She wasn't crazy about having all the guns around them either, but until Evan explained what was going on, and why he was there, it didn't seem prudent to let down their guard.

Lena considered for a few minutes, and then waved at the floor. "You can relax. We know he's not armed, and he can't get out that easily."

The weapons were placed on the ground with only a little complaining.

When people were quiet again and everyone was around the table, Lena straightened in her chair. "Okay, no more excuses. What happened to Abigail? And why are you here?"

CHAPTER TWO

Evan spent most of the journey thinking about how he would answer these questions. When the council sent him, they hadn't given him a formal statement. It was supposed to make him more believable, putting it into his own words, but he wasn't a diplomat. He might just make it worse.

"I guess I should start with Abigail." He rubbed his face, feeling the grit from the road mix with his sweat. "She's the reason we are going out to other communities. Although, yours is the first. We need to get a bit stronger before talking to other groups."

"Stop rambling," Ava said. "What happened to her?"

Lena let Ava take command? Was it because of her schoolmarm attitude? Evan automatically responded to it.

"She's dead," he said. "It happened a few months ago. She just got worse as time passed. We couldn't deal with it any longer. I couldn't be part of it anymore."

Lena glanced at the others in the room. They nodded back, everyone alert. Their guns were near at hand; she hoped they wouldn't be needed. "Abigail tried to make us indebted to the community forever, basically making us slaves. She stole half our rations and we almost died on the way here because of it. She wanted to take our children away. How exactly did she get worse?"

Evan looked at his hands, which were clasped on the table in front of him. The anger and despair at the memory held him back.

"Evan, you have to tell us, so you might as well just say it."

He looked up at her, swallowing the bile in his throat. "After you escaped — yes, we were trying to make you stay no matter your plans — she didn't want to chance losing again. The next group that came, a family, two kids and two dads. She made us put them in the jail and we took their horses and supplies. Once they realized she wasn't going to give them back, they agreed to stay."

"So we escaped, and she used that as an excuse to make it harder to leave? Are we supposed to feel guilty?" Ava asked.

Lena put her hand on Ava's arm. "How many travelers come past?" she asked.

"More these days. We're the first large community people travelling west come to. The cities are failing. The smaller towns are struggling to provide for the inhabitants, so people keep moving on." He stopped speaking for a moment to break what he knew was going to be a list of excuses. "Our community isn't a bad place. There are way worse out there."

"So we're supposed to accept you because you aren't as bad as you could be?" Ava asked.

"No, I'm just trying to explain."

She waved her hands to dismiss his words. "Fine. What happened next?"

He felt the heat of shame warm his cheeks. "The next few groups were the same. Then Abigail said we couldn't take on anyone else. She wanted us to steal the supplies and move the people on. She said it was them or us." He rubbed his face again. "I couldn't do it, so she sent me to the fields. Then I heard she said to kill anyone who came by. Her excuse was they would tell communities down the road about us, and we would be attacked."

"So you killed her?" Lena asked. "That doesn't make me feel like you can be trusted as partners. What happens when we don't agree?"

Her words felt like a slap. "No! We were planning to put her in the jail until we could get her calmed down. She was cool when you saw her, right? By the end, she was ranting. But she got away. I joined one of the search parties. We wanted her gone, but not that way, left to die because she didn't know how to hunt or build a shelter. We wanted her gone, you can understand that, right? We wouldn't kill her."

"It's pretty much what she'd been doing to other people. Why should we believe you are here to make allies, and not to steal what we have?" Ava asked.

Evan felt heat rise in his cheeks again, this time anger, not shame. "All I can say is we've changed. If we wanted to steal your supplies, why would I be here alone? I was the one who found her. She was lying underneath a tree. I thought she was sleeping, but then I saw the blood."

"An animal?" Scott asked.

"A bullet. She'd been shot by someone from the fort. They left a mark, so we would know. They do that with territory markers. They are expanding. Abigail must have run into them. Knowing her, she fought to keep the land in the community."

"So Abigail died. Now what happens to the people she trapped?" Scott's voice was bitter. The Community of Hope had tried to steal his horse and wagon along with their supplies. Evan remembered how Scott seemed to love the animal.

"They all stayed. Like I said, it's not a bad place. They had found friends and purpose, so they didn't want to go on the road again. Especially now that the Fort was stretching its boundaries. And we changed the name. There was too much bad history linked to it. We called the town Prosperity."

"So why are you here?" Lena asked.

"I'm here to ask you to form an alliance with us. We are all weaker than Newton's men. If we work together we might have a chance. You'd get more people here to help defend the farm. We would get access to your knowledge. You've found a way to thrive here. We need to know how to do that. Abigail didn't worry about what skills people had when she trapped them, so we don't have what we need."

It was clear that Lena didn't believe him. He had to admit that the deal was lopsided. The farm stood to gain more from the alliance than Prosperity.

Lena stood up and pointed to Scott. "Put him in Tik's room, it's the most secure. Lock the door."

Evan didn't protest. They needed to talk without him there. He would wait, and he would rest.

"I think he's getting a little better," Pallavi said. She was standing at the far end of the shelter waiting for her father to fall asleep, so she could slip out and get more supplies. Mahir had rushed over as soon as he saw her get close to the secret exit.

"The stew did help," Mahir whispered back. "But you should stay here."

Pallavi bit back the words that surged out of her mind. She was sixteen, and a nine-year-old shouldn't be able to order her around. But there was no room in the shelter for teenage moodiness. This new world made her think about everything she said. She could only hope that Mahir had the same consideration when he became a teenager. If they were still here.

She glanced at her father again; his normally warm dark skin was ashy. And his breathing had a worrying rasp to it. When she touched his forehead earlier, it was hot but there was no fever sweat. He'd dutifully drunk all the water that she passed him. Her hope was, with enough liquid, he would start to sweat, and the sickness would break.

"He needs something more than vegetable stew," she said. "There are medicines, and there were lentils, and rice."

"And how will you explain that? It's easy for him to believe you could grow those vegetables. But he knows how much medicine we brought. And he also knows how much he's taken." Mahir nudged her away from the gap in the shelter wall. "It's too dangerous. There are bad people running around. How do you think Dad will react if you don't come back one day?"

Pallavi hadn't let herself think about that. If she got caught, she would be leaving Mahir alone. Her father wouldn't last long without her care. But he wouldn't last long anyway, and she couldn't let that happen just because it was a little risky. "I'm careful," she said.

"I'm sure everyone thinks they're careful." Mahir's face set with his stubborn look. "Tell me what you're looking for. I can go get it."

"Is it because I'm a girl?" Pallavi regretted the sarcasm in her voice as soon as it was out. "I'm sorry. Look, I'm experienced at this. You need to be trained."

"Then train me. And yes, it's because you're a girl," he said with a shake of his head. "The bad people may be looking for pretty girls."

It hurt Pallavi that her little brother knew about such evil stuff. He'd been so young when the plagues hit. Just old enough to be vaccinated. A few months earlier and he would've died like so many of the other children. She could only think that Dad had told Mahir what he thought the world was like outside. And even though her brother had been out, it hadn't been enough to convince them that Dad was completely wrong. And maybe he wasn't. She'd seen strangers roaming the woods lately. Men in groups of one or two. She'd avoided them so far.

"Stay here with dad, please," she asked. "I don't have time to train you right now. I promise I will. But right now, someone has to watch over Dad."

She put her fingers across her brother's lips as he tried to answer her back. She was losing time by arguing. His fingers clenched in frustration. Then he relaxed.

"Okay, this one time," he said. "But if you don't come back soon, I'm coming for you. And then Dad will be left alone. So you better not stay away too long."

Pallavi leaned against the gap. It was just big enough for her to slip through, but it also allowed her to see if anyone was outside before she left. It was evening, but the sun was still there. If she hurried, she would be back before it was full dark. No matter how urgent the need, being out in the dark was terrifying. Because when she couldn't see, all of Mahir's bad people seemed to be crowding her.

"Okay, I promise I'll be back soon. An hour, that's all I'll need." What she didn't say was if she couldn't find what they needed in the storehouse at the farm, the next trip would have to be days long. Dad had done a lot to prepare them, but it had only been for five years. It had been six since they shut themselves in the shelter. It proved how sick he really was, that he hadn't done the math.

Mahir reached to swing the loose panel to the side until it stopped. Pallavi planted a kiss on his forehead and wiggled through the gap.

CHAPTER THREE

Lena passed the mashed potatoes to Scott. Dinner was usually a fun event with people sharing what happened to them during the day, teasing each other. She was sure that more than one practical joke was planned in whispers during the meal. Tonight, they were silent. Even the kids concentrated on eating. They would have their say, they all would, but Lena had asked them not to all talk at once.

"Are you going to start the conversation?" Scott asked.

Lena had hoped at this point to have her thoughts in order. A decision at least partially formulated. She'd wanted to give the group something to argue against, or support. But she just didn't know. Their history with Evan's community was too raw still. It was only by a tiny slice of luck that they were able to sit around this table now. The problem was, like everything in life, it wasn't that simple. They were too small a community to defend against anyone. And it hadn't been a problem until recently. She had really hoped to have time to pick and choose their allies.

"Okay, I have to be honest," she said. "I don't know what to do. Does anyone?"

She watched as they all reacted to the question. Half of them seemed to be giving a glare to the other half. As though saying, *don't bring up that stupid idea*.

She dug into the food on her plate. There was no way she was going to let them trick her into saying anything more.

"It's risky either way," Keith said. "It could be a trick. He says he's representing that community, and it has changed. That could all be lies. He could be here getting information for the people up the hill. Or Abigail's still around, and she wants the farm."

"It's always going to be a risk," Tik said. "That's why the gangs never hooked up together. They couldn't take that first step. But they were right, at least my boss would have betrayed any alliance. Is that who we are?"

Tik's background with the gang colored the way he looked at the world. He no longer looked over his shoulder waiting for someone to drag them back, but the gang was all he'd known.

"This isn't like that," Mellow said, nudging him. "Most of us are just trying to get through. We have to trust someone." She looked around the table, and a few people nodded.

Lena wasn't hearing anything new. What they said just added to her frustration. Life was supposed to be simple here.

"I know I'm just a kid," Maya said. "But maybe we should be looking at this differently. Remember we were looking for allies, but not just for protection. Is it okay that we change that now?"

Maya was too smart for her age. She was right, they needed more than just protection. The two kids needed friends, and eventually they would need someone to fall in love with. Lena glanced at Ava, who simply smiled. They'd had this conversation enough. Ava used to be a teacher, and she knew more about what kids needed for their future than anyone else in the room. And they were her kids.

"That's a good point, Maya. We need to be very careful about making short-term decisions." Lena pushed her plate away and took a drink of water. "Does anyone have any real ideas, I mean ones that we can act on? If we all agree that it's too risky to do anything, then we've probably lost the battle. And we might as well hand the farm over to the first person who comes knocking."

Deb rolled her eyes, and Lena had to hold herself back from snapping at her.

Even though Deb insisted she wanted to be part of the group, she acted like a sulky teenager. When it got to be too annoying, Keith would have a talk with her and she'd be better for a while. Lena still couldn't understand how Keith and Deb could be married. Or maybe, more precisely, how they could be so happy together.

"Okay, I think we all agree that it's risky either way. That doesn't mean we do nothing. I have an idea," Deb said. She waited while everyone stopped eating and paid full attention to her. "So, before all this shit happened, do you think we didn't have to deal with this kind of problem? I know things are different, but people don't change. It's bigger stakes, but other than that, it's exactly like allowing somebody into your clique."

Lena tried to keep her face open and interested. It pained her to admit that Deb was right. People made alliances from the day they started to socialize. It may not have ended up in real death, but a bad choice could've ended up in social death. "You are the only person here who was part of the in-crowd, Deb. How did you do it?"

Deb smiled. Apparently she'd missed the sarcasm in Lena's words. "We tested anyone who wanted to join us. You noticed it in things like getting on the cheerleading squad. But we did it with everything. So, we make a test. If he passes, we trust him, if he doesn't pass... Well, we'll figure that out based on how he does."

"How do we know if he passed the test?" Tik asked. "I mean, your idea is okay, and better than what we did to initiate gang members, but we need to know if he completed it. And can we spare someone to monitor him?"

"Or risk someone on a test," Lena pointed out. "Did you have something in mind, Deb?"

"It's easy. We don't have to watch him. Part of the test is for him to come back with something. Maybe we send him to Crystal to spy on them. Get us something we can use in negotiation."

"That's not the way to start an alliance," Ava said.

"Maybe we send him to spy on Cole?" Mellow said. "It's dangerous, so it's a good test of his commitment. And he could bring something back to us that proves he was there."

"And we would trust what he told us?" Lena asked.

"It depends on what he tells us," Deb said. "I've had a ton of experience with this kind of thing. We'll know, believe me."

Pallavi stood behind the tree and scanned the secret entrance to the root cellar. It was risky going in so close to the last time. She relied on the fact that if she was still able to get in, then nobody had noticed, and she would be able to keep going. After all, they'd block her out if they knew. And then things would get really bad. Mahir was right that it was dangerous, but she really had no choice.

She could see the lights on in the farmhouse, on the main floor. These people weren't confined behind what was supposed to be an impenetrable barrier. They could leave their house every day, work in the fields, and talk to each other. There had been days when she just stood here watching them, wishing she was part of that family instead.

A dry branch cracked behind her. She spun around and saw her brother creeping up. As much as she wanted to yell at him, she waited until he was standing beside her.

"You are supposed to be watching Dad," she whispered. "We can't leave him alone too long. He'll figure out that we're leaving."

Mahir glared at her, then glanced over at the two buildings.

"He's sleeping. I know he's sick, and I know you have to do this, but you need to let me help."

Her brother's talent for persistence had never been cute. Well, maybe to her dad. Pallavi learned a long time ago that her capacity for patience was nowhere near enough to outlast him when he was determined to get his way.

"So, what's your suggestion?" She glanced over her shoulder at the house and the root cellar again. There was no one around. She took Mahir's arm and dragged him away and into the stand of trees at the edge of a field. There was no way this argument was going to stay quiet enough to be this close to the other people. "Dad's sick and we don't have enough supplies. These people have what we need. And they don't seem to notice when things go missing. I get it, it's risky. But what are the options? Give me your ideas." Part of her felt good at getting it all out. It was hard to be the one to make these decisions. Hard to be the one to take all the risks. The other part of her, maybe the biggest part, felt bad. It wasn't Mahir's fault that they were in this position. It really wasn't anyone's fault, but Dad was a bit to blame. If he hadn't been so paranoid, they might be living in the farmhouse, or somewhere like it.

"I don't have any better ideas," Mahir said. His fists were clenched, and there were tears ready to fall. "I just know that there are bad people out here too. I just don't want you to become one of them. Stealing is how it starts, and then you kill someone."

It hadn't occurred to Pallavi that Mahir thought she would step over that line. It wasn't something she thought about. And maybe that made Mahir right. Not thinking about things like where the line was was the first step to crossing it, and not noticing until you looked back and saw it in the distance. Then it would be too late.

"I wouldn't do that," she said.

Mahir looked down at his shoes. "How do you know?" His voice was small.

"I just do." She knew that Mahir was looking for reassurance, but she had none to give. Dad was sick, probably dying. She was stealing medicine from people who might need it, knowing full well that it probably wouldn't make any difference to Dad. If Mahir got sick, how far would she go to save him? The fight went out of her, and she pulled Mahir into a hug.

"Maybe Dad just needs some meat, like you said." Mahir looked off to his right. "There's a river here, I've watched fish going by. It would be way less risky to catch some fish."

She was thankful that Mahir didn't realize how sick their dad was.

"How are we going to explain fish? We don't have a pond."

Mahir giggled. "We don't have a garden either." He grabbed her hand and started pulling her towards the river. "We'll think of something. I don't think Dad is really that interested in picking apart our stories. At least, as long as you make tasty food from them."

Pallavi chuckled. "So, you mean as long as I do the cooking. Okay, let's get some fish. You will clean them here. I will figure out what to say to Dad."

Mahir grinned and hurried toward the river. He'd gone from an emotional wreck to a kid in a flash. She hoped that he would keep that ability, but knew it was unlikely; the world was not going to get kinder.

Pallavi followed her brother, keeping alert for any other sounds. It may be less risky to catch fish, but it would take longer than stealing a few medications.

CHAPTER FOUR

They were talking it over. Evan couldn't hear the words, but every few minutes voices were raised. Not a fight, but a passionate discussion. If the situation was reversed, would Prosperity be any more trusting of an old enemy?

The door swung slowly open. The boy, Jason, stuck his head in and nodded when he saw Evan sitting near the window. He entered the room, closing the door behind him after a quick glance down the hall.

Jason was here without permission; that might work in his favor.

"Aren't you part of the discussion?" Evan asked. "I thought everyone had a say here."

Jason shrugged, his nonchalance denied by the frown. "They aren't ready to make a decision yet, and I don't need to listen to the debate."

"You've already made up your mind?"

Jason sat on the edge of the bed and looked at Evan intently. "I know what they are talking about, but I need to know your story more before I decide. It doesn't seem right that they suspect stuff and won't give you a chance to talk." He leaned back against the headboard, putting his feet on the bed. "How do you see this working?"

"The alliance?" When Jason nodded, Evan continued. "It's not so simple. I'm not in charge at Prosperity, so maybe they have an agreement all ready, but I'm guessing it will be a negotiation."

Jason looked out of the window for a few minutes. "You said it was to defend against the people in the Fort. How will that part work?"

This time Evan heard fear in Jason's voice. He guessed it wasn't fear of the fight; Jason had been just as quick as the adults in raising his gun. It was about who he might lose. "We would make sure that both Prosperity and the farm are well defended."

Jason sat up again. His cheeks reddened with some emotion that Evan couldn't name.

"I'm not a kid," Jason said. "I'm tired of people thinking I can't work out real problems." He drew in a deep breath, getting rid of some pre-teen rage. "If you are too weak to defend against the Fort, how will you fight against them and help protect us? There are only so many fighters and splitting them between two places will make *us* safer, not you. Any idiot can figure that out."

"Not everyone looks at it like that. And not all of them are idiots," Evan said. He leaned forward and dropped his voice, hoping the closeness would help Jason get control of his anger. "It's not just that. Sure, the Fort is the current threat, but they aren't the only problem. Out here, we need to stick together, or someone will just bully us into everything. I'm guessing that when we agree to an alliance, there will be other towns. The Fort won't attack so easily if they know we'll come running to the fight."

He watched Jason digest that idea. "So, some kind of standing army? We're two days from anyone around here. The Fort attacks and it's over before reinforcements can come."

Evan grinned. "That's why it will be up to the leaders to figure it out right now."

Someone called Jason's name.

"Coming," he yelled back. He slid off the bed and opened the door. "That won't be enough of an answer if they ask the same questions. You need some ideas." He shut the door and thudded downstairs before Evan could reply.

The kid was smart. Evan's focus had been on getting to the farm and convincing them that Prosperity could be trusted. He should have taken the time to figure out some logistics, or asked the council before he left.

He stood at the window and looked across the fields. The crops were partially harvested. If they could agree to cooperate, maybe next year there would be more; they had the land for it. Between Prosperity's farms and this one they could specialize and plant enough to sell to other communities. He might not have a handle on the immediate tactics, but Evan saw the vision. The future was about small communities working together. As a group, they were less of an easy target for people like Newton Cole.

Ava leaned against the kitchen counter, watching as the others tossed ideas around while they cleaned the dishes. She had her thoughts, but was willing to let other people share theirs before offering a solution. And the missing supplies continued to niggle in the back of her mind. She couldn't quite put her finger on it, so she couldn't explain it to the others, but she was sure that things were taken, not just missing. Who would've stolen from them was as much a mystery as the stealing.

"That's not significant enough," Scott said in response to the latest suggestion. "If he doesn't have to put himself at risk, it's not really a test."

Lena patted his shoulder. "We've come so far," she said. "I don't know if I like the fact that now we're focused on testing people. When we all met, were we just stupidly naïve and very lucky?"

Scott leaned over and kissed her cheek. "Yes, but when we met, you were running away from the city, and I was just a wanderer. I know it was just a year ago, but the world has changed. And we have history with Evan."

Keith placed the last of the cutlery in the drawer and gave it a shove, not quite slamming it. "We have to decide on something. And we can't ask him to do something so dangerous that he won't trust us enough afterward."

They had been going over the same argument for an hour, and Ava was getting anxious to talk about the supplies. She pushed away from the counter and took a chair at the table. She bumped a few elbows in the process; the kitchen was large, but the designer hadn't anticipated this many people in it at the same time. "Here's a problem," she said. "None of us are wrong, and all of the ideas are tests. But we must settle on something, and I have an idea."

The others stopped their milling around and focused on her. Ava figured she'd never forget her classroom management skills. And frankly, she figured they came in handy more now that they were here on the farm trying to run it is a collaborative effort. Collaboration was great in theory, but until they got better at it, it wasted a lot of time.

Lena crossed her arms and nodded. "I was wondering when you'd get around to telling us. You were always better than me at pop quizzes."

Ava remembered when they both taught school. Those last few years it had been an exercise in futility as more children left school early.

"The one thing that we haven't done yet is find out how big a threat the Fort is. It would be dangerous for Evan to scout them out, but it would be a good test. He'd be putting his life on the line, but it would be for his community as well as ours."

Tik put his arm around Mellow. Ava noticed he did that anytime he was feeling a little unsure. And he felt that way quite often when he was going to contradict, or suggest something to the group. Over the year, the behavior he'd learned from the gang had faded, but he still struggled with real confidence instead of bravado.

"Can we spare someone to go with him?" Tik asked. "If we don't have a witness, how do we know that he's completed the test? Or if he's telling the truth. A test is no good if we don't believe he's passed it."

Ava looked around the room. "I don't think we can spare anybody. I mean, until he's passed the test, can we trust him not to attack anyone that we send?"

"There's nothing we can do about it," Lena said. "Right now, we can't put anyone at risk. If Evan passes the test, we won't have to send a witness. If we put someone at risk it will be to strengthen us, not just to get information. Then if Evan goes, it will be as a partner, not a prisoner. Are we agreed on that?"

"Yeah," Ava said. "We should probably agree on that. He passes the test and it's done. We can't keep asking him to prove himself."

She watched as everyone nodded or otherwise give their agreement. "Good, then let's just finalize the details."

Pallavi dipped the spoon into the bowl of rice and fish again. Dad had only eaten a couple of mouthfuls. It wasn't enough to help him get better.

"Daughter, I've had enough. You eat the rest; you're too skinny." He coughed, and then started gasping for breath. His body shook with the effort to clear his lungs.

Pallavi bit the inside of her cheek to stop the tears. She didn't speak, letting him gain control before presenting him with another spoonful.

"I said, I've had enough." His voice was too weak to carry any emotion, and her father had never been the kind to rebuke her.

He sighed and added. "It tastes wonderful. Where did you get the fish? I didn't think we had any."

Pallavi glanced at Mahir, who looked away. Like so many other things these days, he hadn't agreed with her choice of lie. "We dried some, remember?" Taking advantage of his weakened state and how it affected his memory seemed cruel, but Pallavi couldn't tell him the truth. If her dad knew that she'd gone outside, he would only waste energy worrying about her anytime she wasn't in sight. "We were worried that there wouldn't be enough protein, and drying fish seemed to be the smartest idea."

She heard her brother rise from the crate he'd been sitting on. He wouldn't argue with her, but it seemed he also couldn't sit in the room while she told the lie. The only other room in the shelter was small, but gave some semblance of privacy to whoever was using it.

"Just one more taste, Daddy," she wheedled. "You need to get stronger. And I don't need to get fat."

A chuckle turned into another coughing fit. Pallavi's heart froze. The sound of his struggles for breath were causing pain in her own chest. She couldn't imagine her father being healthy again. Neither could she imagine life without him. She couldn't stay in the shelter if he was gone, but Mahir had a point: it was dangerous outside.

"It would be hard for you to get fat on the little food we have. I should have thought ahead more," her father whispered. He nodded his head at the spoon, and opened his mouth.

Pallavi raised a smile as he chewed. She tried not to notice how dull his skin looked; almost white, where, in health, it was usually a glowing brown. She blinked, trying not to upset him with her tears.

"I will sleep now, daughter," he said after swallowing the last morsel. "I will feel better when I wake up. I promise."

He rolled onto his side and pulled the thin shawl around his

shoulders, closing his eyes and relaxing into sleep almost imme-
diately.

Pallavi looked at the bowl in her hand — only four spoonfuls
gone. Her own appetite had faded as she watched her father.
Mahir was always hungry; the food would not go to waste.

She placed the cloth across the top of the bowl, waiting for
Mahir to come out of the room. They were going to have the
same argument; she wouldn't let him win this time. There were
medicines in that storage room, and her father needed them. She
wasn't going to let him die just because she was afraid to take a
little risk.

CHAPTER FIVE

Evan followed Scott downstairs. It had been a long day, and everything was starting to weigh on him. Whatever the test was, he hoped it would give him time for some rest before he started. Waiting for their decision had been more stressful than he'd expected. He hardly slept last night, jumping at every creak and murmur he heard. It was so quiet on the farm at night that any tiny sound was amplified.

This time, there were only a couple of people in the room. Scott pointed to a chair and then went to sit beside Lena. Ava sat on Lena's other side. It felt like he was facing a panel of judges, and they all looked at him with blank expressions.

He made himself comfortable on the kitchen chair and smiled, hoping it would hide how nervous he felt inside. It didn't make any difference to their faces. Maybe they just couldn't forgive what happened, and they were about to tell him to go back to Prosperity. Those weren't his orders. If he was unsuccessful at the farm, Evan was supposed to go to one of the other communities in the area. But the farm was what they really wanted to be their first alliance. It would put them both on a more equal footing, and hopefully present them as assets in future negotiations. As much as he hated to admit it, the people on the farm had good reputations and Prosperity needed that to balance out their past.

Evan cleared his throat, not willing to be the first one to speak. The power was in their hands. He awaited their decision, not the other way around.

"I guess we should just get to it," Lena said.

Evan straightened a little in the chair.

"We do see the value in your proposition. But you know we can't just jump into a partnership — no one would with your town's history." She glanced at the people on either side. It made Evan think that perhaps there was dissent. "We've come up with a test. Would you agree to perform it?"

"Do I get to know what it is before I have to answer?" *Or is this part of the test?*

"Don't you trust us to come up with something that you'll survive?" Ava asked, leaning forward.

Her words answered his unspoken question. Whether they knew it or not, these people had been testing him from the minute they saw him. "It's not that," he said. "It wouldn't make any sense for you to give me a test that killed me. It would just cause problems between Prosperity and the farm. I'm just wondering if it's something I *can* do, rather than something I *want to* do. I'm happy to take your test, as long as I have the ability."

Ava sat back, apparently satisfied with his answer. She nodded to Lena, and then turned to face Evan. An itch started between Evan's shoulder blades. This was going to be dangerous, and he wasn't sure anymore if they wanted him to succeed. Something about the way their eyes focused on him was unnerving. As though they expected to read his thoughts.

"Don't worry, you have the skills," Lena assured him. "In fact, most of us have the skill to do what we ask you. But it's dangerous, and we can't risk anyone."

"How will you know I've accomplished the goal? Someone

coming with me? I assume this test isn't something that can be done on the farm." He had a sinking feeling that they were going to send him to the Fort to kill Newton Cole.

"You'll go alone," Lena said. "You'll be able to prove that you completed the task."

"Are you going to tell me what it is?" he asked. "Or am I supposed to guess?"

He noticed a smile pull at Scott's grim expression. He had an ally in this game of power, at least for now.

"You're going to the Fort—"

"I'm not killing anyone," Evan said before Lena could finish. "I won't do it, and it won't help anyway."

Lena looked shocked, and then suddenly waved her hand to dismiss what he said. "Not asking you to kill anyone. We need knowledge whether or not we form an alliance. You'll go to the Fort, you'll gather something that will prove you were there, and you'll bring back some kind of intelligence to help us deal with them."

"So, I'm your spy?" Evan wasn't turning the test down, spying would help Prosperity too. "How will you know I'm not lying?"

Lena looked at him for a moment before answering, as if she was trying to see inside his mind, all the way to his conscience. "You'll have to find something that convinces us of your veracity. I don't know what to tell you to bring without knowing what's there at the Fort."

"I guess we'll see what happens," Evan said.

Keith stood, placed his hands on the table and leaned forward. "No, here's what we'll see. You come back with something that convinces us, or don't come back. And if you don't come back, be ready to run if I see you around."

In the back of the shelter, over the bucket of filtered rainwater, Pallavi washed the dishes. Last night, Mahir had emptied the bowl of food that her father hadn't been able to eat. He looked guilty when he ate, but at his age he needed fuel, and they couldn't afford to waste food. She wiped the tears that were falling now that her father was unable to see them. He still slept, but his breathing was harsh and labored.

There was no choice now but to go for the medicine, and hope that it would work. She knew some of it was antibiotic, and that cured most things. The trick was to slip away without Mahir knowing to avoid the argument, or the offer of aid. If she could wait for night, it would be easier to slip out, but very hard to find her way to the farm. At night landmarks looked wrong. And she risked getting lost at best, or meeting the wrong kind of person at worst.

"You're going out, aren't you?"

Pallavi drew in a sharp breath. How had Mahir become so good at sneaking up on her? Perhaps it wasn't him, perhaps she had been too deep in her own thoughts to hear him. She would have to be alert when she went. "Dad's not going to get better without medicine." She wasn't going to defend her actions and give her brother something to hang on to for an argument. "You need to stay here in case he wakes up."

Mahir glanced back at their father, who was curled up on the couch, sweat beading his forehead. The sweat hadn't brought the relief that Pallavi had hoped for. "He's not going to wake up soon. You need a lookout."

His matter-of-fact statement was worse than argument. Her brother was too young to face this stuff. *No, that's old-world thinking, and the old world is gone.* Mahir should be facing this stuff and learning how to survive it. "He's too vulnerable. If an animal gets in here, and he's alone, we could come back and find him dead."

Mahir blinked and Pallavi saw the moisture in his eyes. He knew that their dad was dying, but she wouldn't talk about it with him; talking about it made it real.

"And if you get caught?" Mahir said. "There's no one to take care of him. I don't know what to do. You are the one who makes us better when we're sick. Like Mom used to."

If Mom were here, Pallavi thought, she'd know how to talk Dad into leaving the shelter. "I won't get caught. I know what I'm doing. You have to trust me." Pallavi hoped Mahir would believe the words even if she didn't. "You know where I'm going; it will take me a while to sneak in. That's why I usually go in the evening, when they're not paying attention. But now people will be on the farm walking around, and I might have to wait."

"So, wait till evening," Mahir begged. "You won't be gone so long. I won't have to worry so much."

Pallavi put the cloth she was using to wipe the dishes on the small counter. She pulled Mahir into a hug — he only gave a little resistance — and kissed the top of his head. "I know. But if I go now, maybe I can get in sooner than evening. Then I'll be back, and Dad might be getting better before sunset."

Mahir hugged her tight, and then, speaking into her chest, in a small voice, asked, "Is Dad going to get better? Is it worth it for you to risk your life?"

Pallavi untangled herself from her brother, and held him out at arm's length. She lifted his chin so he would look in her eyes. "Don't be so dramatic, little brother. Dad's just sick, and I'll only be gone for a little while."

She couldn't tell if he believed her lies, but he nodded and pulled away to sit on the chair beside their dad.

CHAPTER SIX

Not as bad as he'd anticipated. But he wasn't going up to the Fort without some guarantee that, if he did his part, they would do theirs. He shifted in the seat and released the tension in his shoulders to stall for a little time. They were looking at him, clearly waiting for a response. *This is the diplomatic part*. He could just say yes, and head out, but it didn't feel like enough; they both needed some skin in this game.

"What kind of thing can I bring back that would be specific to the Fort?"

Lena shrugged. "I'm sure you'll figure something out when you get up there. Without knowing what they have, it's hard for us to be specific."

They were not going to make this easy. "And what kind of intelligence do you want?" Evan kept his statements short, so he wouldn't ramble and say something that would put them on alert. This group took suspicion to a whole new level.

"You say they're getting ready to attack?" Scott asked.

"We think they are," Evan said. "There's no guarantee that they're going to be doing it in the next while, but it's inevitable.

There's a lot of people there, they don't really have any farmland, and we all know scavenging for supplies is getting pretty hard."

"Well, your trip will give us an indication of how close they are," Lena said. "And, Evan, you have to know that this is valuable information. For both of us. If we have time, then we will be stronger when they do eventually come out to fight. But if they're getting ready, we have to move fast."

Evan nodded. They were right: any information might make the difference between losing a surprise attack, and fighting to, if not a win, a draw. "Are you going to let me take my horse?"

"If you think that will help," Scott said. "It won't take you much more time to get there on foot, and maybe on foot you'll be more able to hide."

It was going to take him most of the day to get there, horse or not. It was hilly ground and maybe he could make better time on foot. Scott was right. He'd have to tether the horse somewhere, and that might give away his presence at the Fort. There were plenty of places where it would be hard to hide the animal, and Cole seemed to be the only person who had horses to spare. "You'll take care of her, right? If I don't come back, you'll find some way to get her back to Prosperity?"

"If we can," Lena said. "If you don't come back, and the people from the Fort attack, we can't spare anyone to go to Prosperity just to return the horse. But we'll look after her, and if we can, we'll send her back."

"How long do I have to complete the test?"

Scott looked at Lena, then at Ava. It looked like they hadn't thought about that part of the test.

Lena stood. "You have a couple of days. If you're not back by then we will assume you are dead, or have joined the Fort."

So, no rescue would be coming. Not a surprise. "It won't take that long. I'm not planning to visit and have tea. I'll leave here as soon as I can, and if I'm not back within one day, just assume I'm dead.

Joining the Fort is not my way. No matter what you think about Prosperity, we are more civilized than that."

He stood and nodded at Lena. "Any chance I can get some supplies, at least some water?"

"Yes. We have some travel rations as well. Good luck."

Pallavi stood poised to run to the store room. She could see the medicines in her mind. There would be no delay. She would get in and out. It was still afternoon, and this was the first time she'd gone in daylight. No one was around. It was unusual and probably wouldn't last, but it was too good an opportunity to pass up.

Mahir was behind her. He'd started his argument again when she prepared to leave. She gave up trying to get him to stay in the shelter and settled for having him for a look out. "You can see everything from here," she said. "I'll be gone only a few minutes."

"How will I let you know if someone is coming?" He leaned around her to stare across the open ground to the entrance to the root cellar. "I can't yell. I should just come with you and stand guard when you go in."

She ground her teeth, frustrated with her brother and the world. If Mahir would just listen to her, she could have finished this already. "I'm going in the back, you won't be able to see what's going on. If someone comes, they will enter through that door." She pointed to the steps. "I'll hear them soon enough."

The clump of trees ended about a hundred yards from the cellar. The official entrance was a few steps down to a door, the passage sheltered under a roof. The storage was partly above ground and her entrance was through a gap in the wall at the back that was hidden by a scrubby bush.

"How do you know this medicine will work?" Mahir asked for what felt like the hundredth time. "Maybe it will make Dad worse."

She closed her eyes and took a breath. They couldn't fight out here without someone hearing. "If we do nothing, he will get worse. I would rather do something that might help. How would you feel if we did nothing and he died?" She hadn't meant to say that. Speaking about Dad dying felt like she was asking the universe to make it happen.

"How will you feel if he dies after the medicine?"

"If he dies, I'll feel bad. But I have to try, Mahir." She blinked back tears. This was wasting time.

"Be careful," he said. "I don't want to be left alone."

She wanted to reach out and hug him. Instead, Pallavi ran to the back of the short building and ducked under the bush. She carefully slid the broken slat aside and slipped into the cool, dim cellar.

The medicines were in the middle of the cellar, protected from a quick glance by crates and sacks of food. Three bottles were labeled amoxicillin. They must have been scavenged from a pharmacy because each one contained hundreds of pills. Pallavi opened all three and took ten pills from each bottle so that it was less obvious that some were missing. Thirty pills must be enough; three pills a day for ten days. The medical book recommended two pills a day, but Pallavi wasn't taking any chances.

She capped the bottles and placed them back in the exact positions they were in before. She swung around and jerked as her hair caught on the rough shelving material. Gently pulling her hair away from the splintered wood, she made sure to retrieve all the broken strands. No need to leave evidence that anyone had been there. Shoving the torn strands into her pocket along with the pills, Pallavi pulled her hair back into a ponytail and tucked it into the back of her shirt.

Time was slipping away. She darted back to the broken slat and left the root cellar. Glancing to see Mahir waving to her, she ran to join him in the cover of the trees.

.   .   .

They could have sent someone to help him on the road, Evan thought as he dodged another thorn bush. Being on foot gave him the opportunity to take a few shortcuts, but not having someone check his back slowed him down too much. This was just on the outer reaches of what he thought of as fort territory.

On the other hand, he only had to worry about himself on this trip. The idea of spying on Newton Cole's men tied him in knots. If they caught him, it wouldn't be just death. They would want some intelligence of their own, and Evan wasn't sure how long he would be able to keep quiet if it came to torture.

Get a grip. All of this is in your head. He'd never been near the Fort, but they were definitely getting ready to expand. There had been enough raids to prove that.

He stood on the top of a rise, hidden by the trees that crowded together in the small patch of dirt in the middle of the rocky ground. He was halfway there, and the climb had him grunting and sweating already. Evan leaned against one of the trees and sank to sit on a protruding root. It made sense to get his breath back, and think about his plan. He grinned at his own thoughts. *Yeah, you're not exhausted, you are being strategic.*

If he came back with good information, Evan reasoned, the proof was less critical. Getting inside to learn their plans was the main barrier. Even at night, even when the guards might be lazy, he couldn't just walk in and ask, 'what's up?'

His best bet was probably to find a place to observe before jumping in to complete the task.

Five more minutes. The heat was not helping either. *When did I get so old? Is this what life is going to be now? Short and hard?* He pulled out his water container and downed half of it. *Maybe the new alliances will work and make life easier.*

Five minutes passed, and another five. The sun moved far enough in its arc to put Evan in the shade, cooling him. It was quiet and peaceful here. A bird soared and floated in the thermals high above. Probably an eagle by the size, he thought. At least not a buzzard, so nothing dead in the neighborhood.

The quiet was doing its magic and Evan felt his eyes drooping. He jerked awake and pushed himself up ready to start his trek again. By dark he should be able to see the Fort and find a place to observe.

The eagle screamed above him, and another call answered. Animals didn't care about what happened to humans. They were thriving. More game meant more food for the predators. And that meant more predators. The sight of the eagle reminded Evan that Cole's men were not the only predators he needed to avoid. Bears would be out soon looking for food before hibernation.

The path wound around the hill. The Fort was accessible by road, but the cross-country paths were still new and mostly formed by animals. They made for great walks on days when you wanted some slow exercise. When you were on a mission, you wanted a fast route. Evan stuck with the path because every time he stepped off, he got stuck in brambles or found a canyon blocking his way. Animals were smarter than humans when it came to getting around.

CHAPTER SEVEN

An hour later, Evan slowed. He was getting near the Fort and didn't want to stumble into view. The sun was almost down, but it was still too light to hide him on the path.

"I told you."

The words came from behind him. Evan looked around; no one in sight yet. This high, the trees were too small to climb, so he stepped off the path into the shadow of the boulders that lay at the bottom of a sheer cliff face. None of them were large enough for him to stand behind, but he could lay on the ground in the shadows behind some of the larger ones. If he didn't move, and the people coming up the path didn't look too closely, he would be safe.

There were mumbled words, but no one spoke as loud as the first person. It took a few minutes for them to get close enough for Evan to hear what they were saying. From his position in the rocks, he hoped to be able to see them as they passed.

"None of the towns around here are ready to defend themselves," the same voice announced. "We should report to Cole now. If he wants us to look farther out, he'll tell us."

"It would be nice to sleep in my bed," the other man said.

They came into sight. Not from behind him, but from a side path. Evan went cold with fear of what might have happened if he'd been five minutes later arriving. In his head, he pleaded with them to move on and to continue to reconnoiter. If they went back to the Fort, he would be delayed. There was too much risk involved in trailing them down the same path.

"He did say just check that farm and the closest town." The first man sounded just as hopeful for his bed.

"We'll get a hot meal at least. Even if he sends us back out. We'll only waste an hour or two."

The first man slapped his companion on the back and they headed down the path to the Fort.

Evan waited until he was sure they were far enough away before rising from the stones.

Was this enough intelligence for Lena? It just proved what he was saying. And those men had been at the farm, not just poking around the area.

It didn't feel like enough.

He didn't have the proof that he'd gone to the Fort. Would that mean they wouldn't believe him? Maybe he shouldn't have been an idiot and cut his time down; a few extra hours would be helpful.

As he sat worrying at the decision, the sun dropped below the horizon and the night animals started their activity. The first to wake were the bugs. They swarmed him, biting at his exposed skin.

Evan grunted and stood. Movement would help, and he couldn't risk the people at the farm thinking his information was invalid. If he was careful, he should be able to carry on — unless there were more patrols on side paths.

The men were going to the Fort, and he wasn't. A place to overlook it would give him time to figure out his next move. And maybe that move would keep him outside the walls.

· · ·

It was late when Ava finally had a chance to go back to the root cellar and double-check her suspicions. This time she was going to check not just the food, but everything. It wouldn't take that long; it wasn't like they had a lot of stuff.

She took a lantern with her. It was dimly lit in there during the day, and at night it was as black as hell. And she didn't want to be questioning her inventory. This time she was going to Lena with proof, or she was just going to let it go.

Even with the lantern, the root cellar was eerie at night. She kept waiting for a spider to land on her shoulder, or a mouse to run across her toes. No matter that she didn't smell vermin, or that there was very little evidence of spiders; the space between her shoulder blades still tickled as if she was being watched.

She set the lantern in the center of the short row of shelving. And then she dug her ledger out of her pocket and placed it on a space in front of her. They still hadn't replaced the crates that were damaged. Evan's arrival had interrupted that work. Ava wasn't planning to spend the night tapping slats back into place. Or re-crating any vegetables. But tomorrow; tomorrow she would make sure it was done.

The shelf in front of her contained stacks of canned food that they scavenged from a grocery store a couple of days away from them, and plastic-wrapped boxes of cereal. Even though mice might come in for the grains, it was nice to have a supply on hand. And so far, the plastic wrapping had held. She counted the cans of salmon and checked them to the ledger. There were two cans missing. She continued through cans of beans, tomatoes, and chili. Each type had two or three cans missing according to the inventory. This food was meant for use when they traveled. And no one had touched it for a long time, so there was no knowing how long things had been missing.

Ava wanted to go and bring Lena in and show her what she'd already found, but it made more sense to continue so that Lena could see exactly what was going on. If it was only a matter of a few travel cans, it might not be enough to convince her.

There was a sack of rice missing. That was harder to explain away. The cans might've been taken for lunch on one of the long harvest days. The contents were cooked so, unappetizing as it might be, eating them cold was possible. Rice needed to be cooked.

By the time she was at their precious box of medicines, Ava was convinced someone was stealing. She checked the cough syrup; it was all there. The rubbing alcohol was all sealed. The bandages were accounted for. All the bottles of antibiotics were open and altogether there were thirty pills missing. Rats would not have unsealed the bottles and then replaced the lids. In Ava's mind, there was no doubt someone was stealing. The trick was going to be figuring out who. The only person who had appeared in their life recently was Evan. It was hard to believe that he was responsible. It would be hard to hide the stuff. And it would've been pretty obvious if he'd removed it in the last day. Her stomach dropped at the thought that it was one of their party, but who else? They had neighbors, but none of them knew about the stores they kept.

She made the final notes, closed her book, picked up her lantern, and returned to the farmhouse, where Lena was on the porch sipping iced tea and staring out over the view. It was one of her favorite things to do before going to bed. Ava hope she wasn't about to spoil that ritual.

"Is there any whiskey in that tea?" Any strength in her drink might soften the blow.

"We don't have enough for me to waste it that way," Lena said. "Maybe we should set up a still, it would be nice to have a party once in a while. And it's probably more reliable than trying to make a good wine. Although, maybe that'll be a benefit from our alliance. We could all specialize in different spirits. And maybe a little weed."

Ava smiled at the idea of them sitting around stoned. "I have some bad news." She waited until Lena put down her glass. "Things are missing." She explained what she found in the root cellar. "I don't know how far it goes," she added. "Someone may be milking the cows early, taking stuff from the field, I don't know what else."

"You think it was Evan?"

Ava shook her head. "Unless he's been hanging around and we haven't noticed, I don't know how he could be responsible for all of it. Maybe some. Maybe the meds, but the food? My gut says it's been going a little bit over time."

Lena looked at her glass. "I guess I should be glad I haven't been sipping whiskey," she said quietly. "So, how bad is it?"

Ava looked at her notes again before answering. "As long as no one gets sick, the meds aren't that important. And, to be honest, they are going to expire soon anyway. I mean, they would have some effectiveness, but not as much as we would hope. The food worries me more."

Lena reached for the notebook and scanned the page. "It doesn't look like much is missing. I mean, yeah, stuff is gone, but the farm's doing well."

Ava took the book back. She knew Lena was smart enough to know that it wasn't the immediate need that worried her. Since Lena wasn't in charge of the stores, she might not know how close they were to starvation with stocked shelves. "If it stops, we'll be fine. Whoever it is, if they keep stealing a little at a time, we won't have any reserves. Without reserves, all it will take is one bad harvest, drought, or a major storm. And we'll have to go scavenging again. And there isn't much out there in the immediate neighborhood. So that means we have to go farther and stay away longer. If it comes to that, it won't matter what the Fort has in store for us. We'll just get worse and worse off."

Lena rubbed her temples, frowning. "I'm going to need one of our dwindling supply of painkillers to get rid of the headache, if anything else goes wrong."

CHAPTER EIGHT

"How closely did you look for evidence?" Lena asked.

Ava shrugged. "I was checking inventory, not a crime scene."

Lena put her tea on the table. "Let's go check. We can't just keep guessing, and unfounded suspicions will hurt us."

Lena hated going into the root cellar. It smelled of old vegetables and dirt. Thankfully, the produce didn't taste like that. Some of the stores actually seemed to taste better after a few weeks in the cool dark.

Ava handed her the lantern as they went in. It wasn't the best light to look for clues by, but it was better than waiting until morning and spending a sleepless night stewing over the possibility they had a thief in their midst.

"How are they getting in?" Lena asked.

"Shit, why didn't I think of that?" Ava walked to the wall and started inspecting it. "I guess through the door, if it's someone we know. Most of the wall is below ground. I'm pretty sure they haven't had time to tunnel in."

Lena followed Ava. With only the one lantern, she couldn't do much more than watch.

They arrived at the back corner and it became clear as soon as the light shone on the wooden slats that made up the above ground walls. One slat was askew. They were about eighteen inches wide, so it wouldn't take much for someone to squeeze their way in.

"I guess we can nail this back into place and stop whoever is doing this," Lena said. "At least until they find another way in. I'll go get the tools."

Ava leaned in to inspect the edges. "We can do that later. I'm more interested now in finding out who it is than stopping a midnight raid."

Lena held the lantern close, so they could see the details. There wasn't a thread, or torn piece of clothing, or anything that would help.

"Maybe it would be better to put a guard here and catch them," she said.

Ava moved away from the slat. "Who would you trust? It can't just be you and me. Until we know who, then we won't be able to feel sure about the guard." She looked at Lena. "Well, maybe that's just me."

Lena couldn't deny that she thought the same. "Let's finish the search. We can take the meds inside and see what happens when we leave that entrance available. A few food items won't be much of a problem."

They continued around the shelving, starting from the broken slat and methodically checking the floor and wooden shelving for clues. "They are professional," Lena said. "Maybe it's someone who's traveling the country, scavenging and moving on."

Ava looked up from where she was searching under the lowest shelf. "Like Scott?"

"I guess, but it's not him," Lena said. "I know him. He wouldn't take anything without telling us, or at least me."

Ava nodded as though she wanted to argue but couldn't think of where to start.

"There is nothing here," Lena said. "Let's grab the medicine box and head back into the house. I'll ask Keith to fix the wall tomorrow."

Ava took the box from the shelf and balanced it on her hip, freeing up one arm. In the light of the lantern, a long, wavy strand of dark hair floated to the ground.

Lena stared at Ava, watching the realization bloom in her mind. The only person on the farm with dark hair that length was Maya.

Ave reached for the strand, pinching it between two fingers. "No. It can't be Maya. She helps me in here all the time. She was here the other day, it must have happened then."

Pallavi filled a small glass with water from their supply, noticing the level in the potable water container was dropping. She would have Mahir transfer some from the rain barrel later.

The first dose of the medicine seemed to calm her father, and he'd slept since taking the pill. It wasn't exactly an improvement, but at least he seemed more peaceful. She closed her eyes and sent a small prayer out that this next dose would break his fever. He was so sick now, he didn't even ask where the drug came from.

She moved past the cot where her brother was sleeping, and roused her father. "Daddy, it's time to take your medicine." She kept her voice low, but didn't whisper. She'd learned long ago that a whisper would wake Mahir faster than a shout.

Her father struggled to sit up, but didn't open his eyes. He held out his hand. She noticed it was trembling as she dropped the pills into it. He tossed them back, and then reached for the water glass. As soon as he swallowed the pill, he lay back down. Pallavi covered him with a blanket and smoothed his sweat-soaked hair.

She watched her father until she was sure he was back in a deep sleep. She wiped the tears from her cheeks and went to the kitchen area. She placed the glass for washing, and then went through the supplies they had for breakfast. Early on they would have fresh eggs from their chickens, but the chickens didn't live long. Now, when she could, she took a few from the farm.

"Is it working?" Mahir asked. While she'd been distracted, he'd woken and come to join her.

She squeezed her hands into fists, to stop herself from reacting to the surprise. "It's too soon," she said when she had her voice under control. "I hope so. But I'm worried that I'll have to go get more."

"You can't!" Mahir tugged on her arm. "You were lucky. But that won't always be true. You get caught, and then what will I do?"

She knew he didn't mean it the way it came out. Mahir wasn't that self-centered. But he was worried, and he was right to be. She wished she was like her mother had been. Pallavi remembered always feeling that her mom could solve everything, and make everything better. "If I don't, what will happen to Dad?"

Mahir glanced over to where their father slept. "I don't know." He slumped as if the whole world rested on his shoulders. "What if Dad dies? What if... What if it ends up being just you and me? I mean... I know Dad's old, even for a dad. And I guess I knew he would die before us, but it should be when we're grown up. How will I look after you? Especially since you don't listen to me."

Pallavi turned away to hide the smile. It never occurred to her brother that she would look after him; he was the one who would take charge. She moved some plates around on the counter, stalling for time. Mahir just kept staring at her, waiting for his answer.

"Let's not worry about that," she said. "We'll be fine. We've taken care of ourselves for a long time now."

"No. No, we haven't. Taking care of ourselves isn't about stealing stuff from people who are working hard."

"It is right now," she said. "And we'll figure something out for the future if we have to. Right now, Dad is the most important thing."

"Exactly! So you can't keep going and stealing things, because if you get caught I can't take care of him by myself."

Pallavi looked at her brother. His body was tense, his hands balled into fists, his face screwed up in frustration.

"You don't have to worry about this, Mahir." This conversation had been coming for a while. She had been avoiding it, but in the last year Mahir had reached a stage where he felt stronger and more in charge than he really was. She couldn't put it off any longer, although she wasn't sure if the predawn hours after a sleepless night was the right time to do it.

She put her hands on his shoulders and bent down so that she was eye-to-eye with him. "You don't have to take care of us. You are my little brother, not my big brother. And even if you were, we are in this together."

She felt the tension relax a little in his shoulders, but the determined look on his face remained.

"I know that. But if you keep taking these risks, I will be an only child."

Pallavi knew she would not break through his emotions with logic. She hadn't talked about what would happen if Dad died, but she'd thought it through. Maybe if Mahir knew that there was a plan, it would help. "We'll go to the farm," she said. "They need people, and there are kids. You can have friends. We won't be alone."

"And when we get there, will you tell them about all the things we stole?"

CHAPTER NINE

Newton Cole didn't seem to worry about energy costs. Most of the electricity these days was battery, and they couldn't be recharged. Light mostly came from candles at night, heat from fires or blankets, and anything else took human power. The Fort was lit up like a Friday night football game. Evan scanned the open area for a clue, but there was nothing obviously powering the lights.

He'd found a hill overlooking the enclosure, close enough to see what was going on, far enough that he wouldn't be obvious from his position, flat on his belly. He'd been watching for an hour and nothing stood out as information that would get the people at the farm to trust him. Maybe the way they used power, but without understanding the source, it wasn't really information.

Taking something back was not so much of a problem. There was a huge pile of garbage downwind of the Fort. He'd find something there.

He pulled a notebook out of his pocket. A pencil was stuck in the spiral binding. About the only thing in seemingly endless supply was paper. It didn't degrade as quickly as most things.

Maybe the fact that there are so many people here? No. That wasn't quite right, so many men. He'd only seen a few women walking around armed. There could be others inside, but it was definitely a male community.

He tried to count the individuals, giving up when he realized he'd counted the same person three times. He wrote *at least a hundred men practicing attacks.* As he looked again, the gate opened. The light pollution made it impossible to see beyond a few feet outside the wall. In contrast to the glare inside, the trails and one road leading to the Fort were black. Evan realized he should have heard the wagon coming up and his stomach tightened in a sudden fear that someone had crept up on him while he was so focused on the action. He rolled to his back and looked around. He was alone. His body relaxed, and he rolled over to look at the action again.

The horses were already on their way to the stable. The wagon bed was covered with a tarp that stretched tight. Evan watched as the driver untied one of the corners and reached inside. He tugged and hauled out a teenage boy. The kid hit the ground and lay there flat out until Cole kicked him; he screamed in pain and rolled into a ball. The kick hadn't been hard. It wasn't the first beating; by the way he recoiled from the ball and started coughing the boy had broken ribs.

Cole kept an eye on the boy as the driver pulled three other kids from the wagon.

Evan tensed to stop his body from running to save the kids. His brain said, *you can't help,* but every other part of him wanted to run in there and kill Newton Cole. Taking the teens was bad enough, but bringing them all the way up to the Fort in a sealed wagon... they were lucky to be alive. *Or maybe not so lucky.*

Then Cole whistled. Four boys, maybe twelve at the oldest, ran from the house. They carried automatic weapons and raised them to shoot. The kids on the ground scrambled to find cover. The armed boys laughed and ran off.

He had what he needed. The Fort was conscripting boys for something. Newton Cole was preparing for more than a few raiding parties; he was getting ready for war.

He watched as a doctor examined the boys on the ground and had them moved into a small room at the end of the stable block. There was nothing left to see.

The garbage pile was a little bit out of his way, but Evan couldn't miss that important part of his test. As he crossed the space between his observation post and the refuse, he kept his eye out for guards on the top of the hills. There had been none when he had first lain down to observe, but perhaps, during the darkest hours, they were the most suspicious, and since they were expecting captives, they may be wary of who would follow them up the road. He didn't see anyone observing. A relief since he needed speed over caution if it was at all possible.

The refuse heap stank. It didn't seem as though the men in the Fort cared about any kind of conservation. It was as though they believed that they would be able to scavenge, or steal, whatever they needed forever. Prosperity, and every other community, worked hard to get as much use out of every single thing as they possibly could.

Evan tiptoed around the rotting vegetables, breathing shallowly to try to minimize his gag reflex. There was nothing in the pile that was easily identifiable as part of the Fort. The darkness didn't help, and there was no way he would light a torch and give himself away.

A gate opened in the barricade close to where Evan crouched over the refuse. The small amount of light leaking from inside the Fort was replaced by a glare that had him blinking. A man appeared and yelled profanity at someone inside, but he wasn't looking in Evan's direction. All Evan could do was hold himself as still as death and hope he would survive.

A clank sounded as something landed on the refuse pile close to him. Not too many people would throw away something with that much metal in it, Evan thought.

He closed his eyes tight against the glare so that when it was gone his night vision would come back quickly. Whatever they'd just discarded might be exactly what he needed.

A man inside the Fort laughed loudly; it had a mean ring to it, as though he had been torturing someone. The man outside kicked something at the edge of the pile and then went back in, slamming the gate behind him.

Alone again, Evan counted the seconds until he dared to open his eyes. If they came from the Fort regularly to dispose of things, his time was limited. He opened his eyes and could see the area around him. The man had thrown a box full of broken guns; the weight of them had broken the side of the box as it landed, and they spilled across the heap. Evan reached out and grabbed one of the mangled barrels. Dragging it close, he ran his fingers across what felt like the results of a vice; the barrel was flattened at the end.

Evan wished it was daylight. The lack of illumination was frustrating when he needed to know if this was his proof. Why would Cole and his men be putting guns through a vice? If they had the ability to damage the metal this way, surely they must have a forge and be able to melt them down to be made into something useful.

Time was passing, and he had no answers. Evan took two of the guns and slid them into his belt. He looked around again and saw a discarded hat — a white Stetson.

Perfect.

Cole liked to sport white cowboy hats, as if he was a good guy in a Western and not the dangerous, vicious man that he was in reality. Someone had stomped the hat until it was almost flat. Evan dug it out from under some potato peelings.

He wasn't going to be able to go back at the same pace that he came. This information was too important. If he found out that

Cole had stolen anybody from Prosperity, or from the farm while he was away, he wouldn't forgive himself.

As he cleared the edge of the refuse, Evan stumbled on an overturned can and fell forward, throwing out his hands to break his fall. A shock of pain went through his right hand. He bit his lip to stop from crying out and giving away his position.

Evan stood, made sure he still had both the guns and the hat, and then ran towards the trail as quietly as he could. He kept his injured hand curled into a fist, trying to avoid leaving a trail of blood.

He didn't stop running until he reached a clearing lit by moonlight, so he could examine his hand. Something had gashed the meat of his palm, but there was nothing in it now. Evan heard running water just across the clearing. A stream ran fast at the edge of the line of trees.

He plunged his hand in the ice-cold water, hoping it would wash away any infection. When his hand was numb, he pulled it out of the water and wrapped it in a scrap of cloth that he took from the first-aid pouch everyone carried when they left Prosperity on a mission. He waited to see if blood would seep through and, when he was confident that the bandage would hold, he turned back to the trail and started to run.

CHAPTER TEN

Evan stumbled into the yard at the farm, pausing to lean on the gate and catch his breath. His run back from the Fort had been more a fall; if it hadn't been downhill he didn't think he would've made it. As it was, he'd come back in half the time he'd predicted when he agreed to the task.

His hand was throbbing. The two items he'd taken from the garbage pile weighed on him. He'd almost dropped the guns at one point, they were so heavy. The hat was crushed into the waist of his jeans.

The sun wouldn't be up for at least another hour, but somebody had left a light on in the window of the farmhouse. The moon had been enough source of light in his scramble to come back. Now he just wanted to make his report, get his hand tended to, and sleep.

As soon as his breathing was under control he made his way to the front door. He grabbed the handle and yanked. It didn't open. A locked door wouldn't keep out Cole's men, but it would discourage a scavenger.

He kicked at the door to get their attention.

"Somebody get up. Let me in," he said. In his head, it was a loud shout, sufficient to wake even the deepest sleeper. But what he heard was barely above a whisper, and sounded more like a plea than an order. He leaned against the door, trying to hear if anyone was coming down the stairs — there was no sound. The candle flickered in the window and went out. He took a deep breath trying to chase away the fear that settled on him with the pain. Someone would be here. If he couldn't get them up, he would just lay here on the porch until morning.

He gave the door one more kick. A creak sounded inside the house. He almost cried in relief. The door opened before he could stand back, and he almost fell on the floor of the front room. Maya reached to stop him hitting the rug.

"You weren't supposed to be back until tomorrow morning." She helped him into a chair. "Oh, your hand. I'll get my mom." She ran back up the stairs, yelling for her mother.

Now that he wasn't scrambling to get back to the farm, or hiding from any patrols that might be out looking for trouble, Evan found himself half asleep as he waited. He closed his eyes and laid his head on his arm, jumping back up as the pain reminded him how damaged his body was.

More than just one person was coming down now. Evan opened his eyes to see Ava standing over him. She reached for his hand and then pulled back without touching it. "Oh my God. Get Deb now!" She sent Maya for some mystery box. And someone else for hot water.

Evan tried to get them to listen to him he needed to make his report. Deb stepped into view.

"In a minute. Just relax so we can check you out. How did you get this?" She was wearing gloves and took his hand, gently prodding at the wound.

"It was in the garbage. But I need to tell you what I saw," he managed to say before she pressed harder on his flesh and he cried out.

"We'll need to clean it. Hopefully we're quick enough to stop it going septic." Deb snapped her fingers in front of his face, waking Evan from a stupor. "Did you clean this?"

He nodded. "Just water, in a stream."

Deb reached for something being passed to her. "Hold him down." She turned and put her hand under his chin, so they made eye contact. "This will hurt like hell. I don't know if cleaning in the stream was a good idea or a bad idea. But all we can do is deal with what's in front of us. I'm going to sterilize it, tape it, and wrap it in a bandage we can wait till morning to hear what you have to say. You might not be able to report after I'm finished."

Evan tensed, then screamed as she poured what felt like acid on his wound. His world went gray at the edges. He clenched his teeth and fought to stay conscious. They didn't know what he'd seen; they thought they could wait for his report.

Deb worked fast. Evan was grateful because he was pretty sure that it would have been just as painful if she'd taken her time, but now it was over. He'd managed to stay awake. And the whole farm community was sitting around the table watching him as Deb tied the knot on the bandage.

"You need to know now," he said.

Lena poured something into a glass and handed it to him, "Drink this. Tell us what you can but you're going to need to rest."

He pulled the hat from his waistband and put it on the table. "This is my proof. You've seen Cole, right?"

Keith took the hat and tried to bend it back into shape. "This was his, I'm pretty sure. So, you've been there, I guess."

Relieved that he didn't have to convince them, Evan pulled out the guns. "I don't know why they're destroying them. But they're taking kids. And I think they're turning them into soldiers."

"Like in Africa?" Keith asked. "Boy soldiers? Shit."

Tik picked up one of the guns. "I heard about those boy soldiers. This isn't the same. At least, I don't think it is. But it's no better." He put the guns back down and looked around. "Cole's just a gang leader. He'll try to enlist those kids. If they don't join up, he'll probably kill them. It's what Basso would do."

Evan didn't agree with Tik's assessment, but it was not worth debating right now. "Who's Basso?" Evan knew they all had pasts, but didn't know the details.

"I was in a gang; he was my boss. Anyway, if I'm right, these aren't Cole's guns. They're stealing whatever weapons they can get their hands on. If they destroy their enemy's weapons, there's no defense."

Evan knew that there were small enclaves of people all around. Not everyone had formed into larger groups. So, if Cole was taking their kids and breaking their weapons there wouldn't be much of a fight left. "He's getting ready to attack us. I mean, someone bigger. Someone like the farm, or one of the small towns."

Tik had given up his room again for Evan. The fact that it was needed drove home another problem for Lena: if more people came to live at the farm, or they made alliances, they didn't have room for more people. She'd talk to Scott about it later. Maybe they could build some barracks or something in the barn.

She cracked eggs into the bowl for breakfast. After Evan was settled, almost everyone had gone back to bed. She hadn't been able to rest for worrying that the slightest sound was the first noise before the attack from the Fort. Scott had slept beside her as though he didn't have any cares. As soon as the sun brightened the sky, Lena got to the kitchen to start breakfast. If the aroma of food didn't get the rest of the people up, she would call them right after the eggs were ready.

"What can I do to help?" Ava asked. She stretched out the kinks from the old mattress, like she did every morning. "I swear, the next time we have the opportunity, I'm going to take the wagon and bring us all back new beds."

Lena reached into the drawer, pulled out the bread knife, and passed it to Ava. "Toast. Is anyone else stirring?"

Ava dug into the bread box and pulled out two loaves. "We'll get Mellow to make more bread later today. No one was awake when I got up. We have some privacy if you want to talk."

Lena didn't really want to talk about this, but they'd put the subject off for too long. Last night felt too soon because neither of them had had the opportunity to let what they'd found in the root cellar sink in. And then Evan had shown up. But they couldn't wait any longer. With every pill, antiseptic, and bandage used on Evan, the loss of the supplies weighed heavier and heavier on her. Ava had been right, it wouldn't take much to leave them without anything.

"Have you talked to Maya?" Maybe it wouldn't be an issue. Maybe it had been Maya, and she had a good reason for it.

"Not yet. To be honest, I was too mad last night and every time I thought of asking her, the words that formed in my mind were accusations not questions." Ava attacked the bread as if still venting. "I'll do it today."

Lena knew how easy it would be for today to turn into tomorrow, and then the next day, and then suddenly the problem had been around for too long to deal with it in any other way than fear. "We need to tell everyone. We can't leave it too long. Did you see the way Deb looked at the box when we handed it to her? I'm sure she guessed something was wrong."

"I won't discuss it with everyone until I've talked to Maya. I don't want everyone accusing her. We need to be able to answer the question about her hair being in the room before we give everybody else a shot; it's too important to just throw it out there."

Ava opened the oven and placed slices of bread on the top

rack. She checked to see if more wood was needed and then crouched down to watch them brown.

Lena knew that staring at the bread as it heated wasn't just to make sure it didn't burn; it was also a way to avoid talking. But, they needed to talk, and she wasn't going to let it go. "When are you going to ask Maya? I mean exactly when."

Ava sighed. A year ago, Lena would never have let one of her teenage students get away with that, but she let it go. Ava was her friend, and she was pushing hard enough.

"I'll do it after breakfast." Ava used a potholder to pull the rack forward. She flipped the slices with her fingers. On the third slice, she misjudged and touched the hot metal with her fingertips. "Damn it all to hell!" Ava finished flipping the toast, slid the rack back in, and then ran her fingers under cold water. "Fine. I'll do it right after breakfast."

"Okay. Whatever happens, we're all going to talk about it at lunch. We're not going to accuse anyone, Ava. No matter what happens, if one of our friends took the medicine, they must have had a good reason."

CHAPTER ELEVEN

Ava pushed the food around on her plate; she was hungry, but the anxiety she felt over the coming conversation took the flavor away.

Maya swore she didn't know anything about the missing meds when Ava asked earlier. Ava believed her, or she wanted to believe her daughter wouldn't do anything like that. How would the others react?

"So that's where it stands." Lena finished explaining everything they knew.

To give her credit, Lena hadn't pointed the finger at Maya. She just laid out the facts; things are missing, the meds were now in the house, and they'd found a hair.

Ava glanced at her daughter. She was looking around the table, but there was no guilt on her face. *She probably doesn't imagine anyone suspects her. Well, anyone other than me.*

"Has anyone seen strangers around?" Mellow asked the question of the group, but she looked directly at Keith. If anyone knew anything it would be him; he was out every day hunting.

Ava found herself hoping that he'd seen a stranger with long dark hair, preferably someone who was looking around the root cellar.

"It's not that easy to answer," Keith said. "You've all been out at some point. There's always some stranger about." He looked around. "Maybe we should be asking Evan. He's the one who's been on the road most lately."

"He's still resting," Mellow said. "Given what we've just learned, sleep is probably the only medicine we can afford to give him." She looked at Deb, their official nurse.

"She's right." Deb stood and took her plate. "I don't really have anything to add. I don't go that far from the farm. My time is best used in trying to figure out how bad the situation is with the meds." She left them to go to the kitchen.

When Deb returned to the dining room to head upstairs, Ava took her arm. "They're in my room," she said. She added the specifics quietly. The people around the table needed to know, but if anyone was waiting outside listening she wasn't going to help them steal again.

Ava put her attention back to the table and noticed everyone was still staring at Keith. He was looking at Maya. Ava clenched her fist under the table where no one could see. She wasn't going to fuel suspicions by defending her daughter without cause.

Keith shook his head. "I still say we should ask Evan, but maybe that can wait. Yes, there are always signs of people. I never see them... That's not true. I rarely see anyone, mostly it's small groups. Can't remember being worried that someone was lurking around. But I haven't really been looking."

"Okay," Maya said. "Just to be clear, it's not me."

"No one's thinking that," Mellow said.

"You'd be crazy not to. Don't even pretend that anyone else here has hair like that."

"You're not the only one with hair like that," Ava said. The words tumbled out as if on automatic.

"Look around, Mom. Almost everyone's cut their hair short. Only me and Lena have long dark hair, and Lena's is too curly."

Ava opened her mouth to defend Maya. But Jason started talking first.

"Why would you do it?" He waited but no one had an answer. "None of us need to steal that stuff. If we're hurt, it's ours to use. Only a stranger needs to steal it."

Tik swallowed the last of his sandwich. "Even if it's Maya's hair, it could've gotten there anytime. Does anyone think it was Maya?"

Ava closed her eyes; she was afraid to know.

"Mom?" Maya was looking right at her. "Do you think it was me?"

Ava blushed. No one was showing any indication they suspected Maya.

"No. I trust you." Ava wasn't sure she was telling the truth. Was she just pretending that other people would suspect Maya to cover the fact she did?

"Okay, we'll wait until Evan is rested and will ask him if he has any ideas." Lena stood and started lifting plates. "Who's on cleanup duty with me?"

It seemed like Pallavi spent most of her time standing watching her dad. Her brain told her that he was dying, but she wouldn't listen to that. Every tiny improvement in his breathing, every moment that he didn't moan in his sleep, gave her hope that he was getting better.

Mahir had left a few hours ago, slipping out while she was tending to her father. By the time she'd noticed, he'd been gone so long that there was no point in going after him. But now, she knew what it was like for him waiting for her to come back from a foraging run.

After more than five years in the shelter there wasn't much left to distract her. It didn't need cleaning and, for a change, nothing needed repairing. She busied herself checking the level of their supplies. When she went scavenging again, she would be better off with a list rather than trying to remember what they needed. It wasn't like she could run out to the store and get something they'd forgotten.

The cupboards were pretty bare. When Dad got better, it wouldn't take him long to notice how bad their situation was. They were going to have to talk to him about leaving the shelter. Pallavi dreaded confessing that they had been out, and been lying to him all this time.

A flash of light caught her attention. Mahir came in through their secret entrance.

"Where have you been?" She hissed the words at him, letting her anger and worry power the question.

Mahir shrugged.

This was new. If Dad was healthy, Mahir wouldn't get away with the insolence. But she couldn't stop him, the fight would just disturb Dad.

She looked at his hands, Mahir had nothing. So, not a supply run. "Did you go out just to play? Do you know how dangerous that was?"

Mahir took a glass and filled it with water. He guzzled it down and then wiped his face. "Is it more dangerous for me than for you?"

What was going on? He was too young to be acting like a teenager. Pallavi looked closer at her younger brother. She noticed a tremor in his hand, a bruise forming on his jaw, and a scrape on his leg. She closed her lips around her first questions. At least now she understood Mahir's attitude; he was scared about something. Covering up fear with bravado was an old habit. "Maybe. I've been out so often I know how to take care of myself. It was really dangerous when I started going. Tell me what happened."

He looked down at his injured leg, and gently touched his jaw. She noticed that the tremor was already subsiding.

"I just fell. I was out scouting. We need more medicine for Dad; it's not helping, that stuff you got."

"Did you go back to the farm?" Pallavi felt dizzy with fear. It was too soon to go back there. If the people at the farm already knew the pills were missing, they would be alert. She'd been planning to spy on them tonight, to see if they were acting differently.

"No. I tried to find other places. We can't keep just taking from them, but we might have to. I know that doesn't make any sense, but I couldn't see any other way."

"You weren't gone long enough to search any of the other places."

"No, I'm not stupid. I went up the hill. I climbed a high tree. I saw some other buildings, but their doors were bashed in and I'm pretty sure all of the stuff inside was gone." He kicked the side of the cabinet.

Pallavi reached to comfort him, but he pulled away.

"How are we going to live?" he asked. "It doesn't matter if Dad gets better, we're stuck here, and there are no supplies, and we've been stealing from the only people who might help." All his frustration boiled out, adding volume to his voice.

Pallavi glanced to see if the noise had woken her patient. He still lay asleep on the couch. Turning back to Mahir, Pallavi realized that every word he'd said was true, and were her fears too. But they couldn't change the past.

"It didn't start out that way," she said. "I didn't think of it like stealing. We needed things, and they had so much. Then I guess we started using them like a store."

"And now we can't stop, right?"

Pallavi nodded. She wasn't going to make things sound better than they were any more. "I'll go check on them tonight. You stay here with Dad. If they haven't found out, I'll only take more medicine. After that, we figure out how to deal with the future."

She waited until Mahir wiped his tears and looked at her. "I promise we will survive, Mahir. No matter what, we are going to be okay."

CHAPTER TWELVE

Ava hated not knowing the answers. Evan shed no light on their problem when he got up. Other than to mention it wasn't uncommon to see supplies disappearing if they weren't guarded. Now, they were in the kitchen discussing how to guard their supplies.

"Where would we stand guard?" Jason asked.

Ava almost said, 'you don't have to worry', but, in fact, everyone would be standing guard on their supplies. They couldn't afford to let the kids sit out this duty. And particularly since she was in charge, it wouldn't be fair to let them off the hook.

She grabbed a piece of paper from a drawer in the kitchen and a pencil, and put them on the table. "I think we need to be inside. Until we figure out what's going on, we need twenty-four-hour coverage." She looked around at the group; to be fair, no one said anything, but they were all stretched thin right now. "I know it's gonna be hard. But if we do short shifts it shouldn't be impossible."

"Wouldn't it be easier to bring everything into the basement?" Keith asked. "No matter what you do with the schedule, it's going to get screwed up. If one of us is out scouting, or hunting, we can't come back to stand a two-hour shift on the root cellar. Not trying to be difficult, but you know it's true; it'll fall apart in a day".

Keith was right. Ava admitted to herself this wasn't New Surrey, where they came from; nothing stayed routine on the farm. But they couldn't just let it go. They had to find out who was doing this. "If it comes in the house, it will be permanent. We can't just keep everything we need in the house; we're already packed in tight."

"Whoever it is," Mellow said, "they're not likely doing this during the day. We could all just keep our eye out while we're around the yard."

"Yeah, Mom," Maya said. "So, we only really need to check it out at night. We don't need everyone. Like, I can do after dinner for a couple of hours and then someone can take over."

Ava's instinct was to say no. If something went missing and Maya was alone on guard... *No.* Ava couldn't let that suspicion live.

"Instead of me trying to figure this out," she said, "you guys do it. You know your own schedules. We should probably cover sunset to sunrise." She shoved the pencil and paper toward Mellow. "I'll take the first shift tonight."

Ava headed out the back door of the farm; she needed to go for a walk, be alone, get her head around why she suspected her daughter so much.

"Mom?" Maya ran down the steps and stopped her. "Are you mad at me?"

Ava gave her daughter a hug. "No. I guess I'm just really worried." She drew back and released Maya. "I've got some stuff to do, honey. I'll be back in time to make dinner."

She watched until Maya reentered the house. It hadn't been a lie. Ava wasn't mad at Maya; she was mad at herself.

Since Evan's report, everyone had agreed not to go too far from the house alone. That meant Ava couldn't just go for a walk for a couple of hours, tiring herself out so her mind would be free to explain her suspicions. But there was one place she could go; the little garden that Lena's aunt had kept going over the years. It was protected by a fence of brambles and no one would be able to sneak up on her. She stopped by the toolshed for a hoe and a basket; digging up some crops would be almost as good as a hike.

An hour later, Ava tossed the last twisted carrot into the basket. No one really worked this garden, but nature seemed to just produce anyway.

She stood and stretched out her back. Looking around, she realized she'd cleared about half the garden. They'd use the vegetables over the next couple of days, and she'd suggest they start using this land more purposefully, maybe as a testing ground for any plants they found in the forest, or seeds they scavenged from stores.

She wiped her hands on the back of her jeans then picked up the basket. The produce wasn't the only thing she'd achieved. As she worked, her brain had run scenarios of Maya's behavior in the last few weeks. Her daughter — her sweet, smart daughter — had started becoming rebellious. It had raised up all the memories of the teenagers in her classes over the years. Maya wasn't up to something, she was just growing up.

"Shouldn't he be starting to get better?" Mahir was leaning over Pallavi's shoulder as she tried to get their father to take another dose of medicine.

She watched him swallow the pills and take a sip of water. He didn't open his eyes, and she wasn't even sure if he was aware of what he was doing. She took the water away as her dad curled back up and pulled the blanket over his shoulders.

If he was feeling the need for a blanket when his body felt so hot to her touch, he wasn't improving. "Sometimes it doesn't work that way. Sometimes it's like people get sicker before they get better." She wished she could be more specific; none of her words sounded convincing.

"There was more medicine, right?"

Pallavi placed the glass in the sink. "You mean more of the same, or just more? Because if you meant more of the same there's no point. If this medicine isn't working, then more won't make a difference."

"We have to try," he said, tugging at her arm.

"What happened to 'it's too dangerous?'"

"It is too dangerous, but if we don't do anything then Dad's going to die."

Pallavi was trapped. If she didn't keep finding medicine, her dad was definitely going to die. She'd read in the book he'd packed for medical emergencies that a prolonged fever could weaken the body too much. They didn't have a hospital to take him to for an IV, or any other useful care. If she kept going to the farm, eventually she'd get caught. Then Mahir would be alone, and their dad would die.

"I said I would go tonight. If I go any earlier, I can't sneak in. I'll get whatever medication they have."

"I'll come with you."

Pallavi spun around to face her brother. There was no point both of them getting caught. "You stay here with Dad, you keep putting cool cloths on his head, and you wait for me to come back."

"No. You need someone to watch out for you," Mahir said. Tears slid down his face.

Pallavi took a breath. Her brother wasn't trying to control her, he was trying to make everything work perfectly. That was not possible; there were only three of them. Two of them, really. It wasn't fair that he had to carry all that frustration inside, but she didn't know how to make him stop trying to fix things. She wasn't sure that she wanted him to stop; if he found a solution, then she didn't have to.

"I know, but someone has to stay with Dad. Someone must protect him. He's sick. What if a wild animal got in here?"

The tension seemed to drain from Mahir. She wasn't sure if he bought her story, and her attempt to make him feel more useful than just an unqualified nurse, but she didn't want to come back and find it had all been worth nothing.

He glanced back to the couch and then nodded. "Fine. But be as fast as you can. If you take too long, I will come looking for you. There's no way I'm going to wait here for days worrying if you've been captured."

Pallavi suppressed a smile at the thought of her brother riding to her rescue. And maybe she was wrong, maybe Dad would get better. It would be a few hours before she left. If his fever broke she wouldn't need to go.

When things go back to normal, I will talk Dad into leaving this place, so we won't be in this position ever again.

Maya approached the door to the root cellar. Her mother had been in there since after dinner. It was too soon to relieve her, but they had a visitor. She knocked on the door in the pattern they'd agreed to as a code.

"Mom?" She kept her voice quiet in case the thief was nearby. She wanted to be the person to catch them. It was kind of fun being on guard.

"Over here."

Maya headed towards the back of the root cellar. Her mom was sitting on a barrel with a dim lantern beside her, and she was writing in a notebook.

"They want you back at the house," Maya said. "What are you writing?"

Ava closed the book and placed it on the shelf beside her. "It's a bit boring in here," she said. "So I decided to try and calculate how long everything in here would last us."

Maya reached for the book. "So how long?"

"It will be rotten before we run out of food." Ava took the book back and pointed at her calculations. "We need to find more ways to preserve stuff. Even if we take in more people, we can't eat all of this before it gets unhealthy."

"Maybe sun-drying?" Maya was already thinking through the books they'd brought with them. "I can do some research. But that's good, right? Even with someone taking some of our supplies, we'll be fine."

Ava stood and picked up her lantern. "It's not the food so much... We don't have enough meds to share them around." She handed back the notebook. "Who's the visitor?"

"Someone from Crystal," Maya said. "They have an answer to our offer of alliance. I'll take over here." She was already working out how much of the stored food she could take for experimentation.

Ava kissed her on the forehead and then slipped away.

The cellar was cool and getting cooler. Maya grabbed an empty sack and started filling it with samples from each of the crates. It wasn't too late in the year to test drying vegetables. And she could use the oven as well. It wouldn't even take more wood to heat. She'd try using it after the bread was cooked. It took hours to cool.

Placing the sack beside the barrel, she jerked at the sound of something scratching at the wall. It was definitely not random wind noises.

She dimmed her lantern as low as possible and crept toward the door. She'd go outside and see what was going on. As soon as she could get her heart to stop pounding, she'd catch whoever was trying to get in.

At the door, she placed the lantern on the floor and slowly

pushed the door. Her pulse sounded in her ears. *Stop being stupid! Whoever it is won't hurt you. The others will come right away if you yell.*

She turned the corner of the building and came to a stop. A raccoon was digging at the base of the wall. That explained the damage, but not the meds; and probably not the missing vegetables — there would have been more mess. She picked up a few stones and threw them near the animal. It hissed at her, and then turned and ambled away.

It would be someone's job to keep the raccoon away. Not hers, she'd make sure of that.

She turned to go back to the door. Something moved between two trees. Too big for the raccoon, and not just a shadow.

Maya slipped back into the root cellar. She would catch the thief. And she could make sure they weren't punished too much; if they needed the food, they should have it.

CHAPTER THIRTEEN

Evan sat at the table in the dining room, this time with the farm people, facing two visitors from another town. Apparently the idea of alliances wasn't new to anyone around here. His hand still hurt like hell, but Lena had offered a little moonshine to everyone and that dulled the pain a bit every sip.

He still wasn't clear on the power balance at the farm. Lena seemed to be in control, but everyone actually had a voice in the matter. He wasn't sure how they ever came to a decision.

The envoys from this town, Crystal, seemed formal, or maybe just a little unfriendly. He was guessing the answer was *no*. It just seemed a little weird that they sent two people to deliver that answer.

The woman seemed to be the leader of the two. She had red hair, pale skin with freckles, and arms like a blacksmith. The man looked more like a teacher, his black hair was a little too long, he was painfully thin, and he wore glasses. In the world before, it was harder to judge people by looking at them. Technology made up for all kinds of physical attributes. But now, what a person did tended to show on their bodies.

"Thank you for your hospitality," the woman, Moira, said. "We've come regarding your request for an alliance."

"Are you sure we can't get you something to eat?" Lena asked.

The offer was a delaying tactic, Evan could tell. If it was him, he'd want the answer right away. The longer they delayed the more difficult it would be to deal with, because they would have to shelter these two for the night. No one would send two people out on the road at night even if the Fort wasn't out on raiding parties.

"No need," the man, Joseph, replied. "We had sufficient supplies for the journey here and back." He said it as though to reinforce the fact that they needed nothing from the farm.

Lena let the silence sit for a moment, possibly a power play but more likely, Evan thought, just another delay.

"We might as well hear it," Lena finally said.

Moira nodded, glanced at Joseph, and cleared her throat. Evan started to wonder what was making her nervous.

"We acknowledge the need for alliances," Moira said. "We have discussed your offer in council. I'm sure you can understand that we can't just jump into the first alliance. This will set a precedent for all other negotiations."

Now this is going to be interesting.

Lena took a sip from her glass. Evan admired her ability to drink it without wincing at the burn from the alcohol. "So, you've come with conditions?"

Moira nodded, and glanced at Joseph again. She was the spokesperson, but he seemed to be the power behind her.

And they're worried about trusting us?

"I wouldn't call them conditions. It's not a simple matter of drawing up an agreement between the two of us. Having an alliance with you will have an impact on our ability to join up with anyone else. Our council feels that we should not be just giving away things, and finding out that we are not able to make our own decisions when it comes down to something important."

"Okay, I guess I can understand that." Lena settled back in her chair. "Size disparity between our communities is an issue for all of us. And that will only get worse as we both make alliances to defend all of the communities."

Moira seemed to relax. "I'm glad you see reason."

"We are nothing but reasonable," Lena said. "But before you start, perhaps Evan can explain Prosperity's idea of what these alliances are."

Pallavi hugged tight to the slender trunk of the tree. Was there someone at the root cellar? Something had chased that animal away. But, right now, there was no one in sight.

She waited, hoping that if she remained as still as possible anyone there would eventually move. No one did. So, she crept toward the back of the building, keeping herself alert to any signs that someone was watching.

The board was still loose. She slid it aside only enough to squeeze through. This was the part she always hated; stepping into the dark room backwards. If someone were there, she would be caught before she could do anything about it. As soon as her feet touched the ground, she spun around; she was alone. She took a shaky breath before stepping away from the exit.

She hadn't been this nervous since the first time she broke in. Perhaps she had become too complacent, and this was a good reminder to be careful. She ignored the crates of vegetables; her nerves would not let her spend the time to sort through them. She needed to get the meds and get out. She rounded the corner and noticed the empty space on the shelf where she'd last seen the medication.

"We moved them."

Pallavi froze. How had someone hidden from her?

"You might as well turn around and talk to me," the girl said. "I'm not going to hurt you."

There was nothing in sight she could use as a weapon; if she survived this she would always bring a weapon. Pallavi put up her hands, hoping whoever this girl was wouldn't get jumpy. She turned slowly.

She'd been caught by a girl who must've been the same age as Mahir. She had long black hair that hung in waves past her shoulders. She was skinny, and kind of looked Chinese with dark skin.

"What's your name?" The girl asked. "I'm Maya."

"Why do you need to know my name?" Maybe if she stalled, she could find a way out of the mess.

"Then I can call you by it, instead of just saying 'the thief'. Because that's what you are, right?"

It was, but it hurt to hear the accusation. She did have a good reason. Then, most thieves probably did. Giving her name should be safe enough, it's not like anyone can call her dad, or the police. "I guess. I'm really sorry I stole." She lowered her arms. "My name is Pallavi Kingman."

"Where did you come from?" Maya didn't seem interested in calling for an adult.

Pallavi was grateful for any reprieve from facing real consequences. "We're in a shelter. It's a ways from here."

"My mom is pretty worried about what you've been taking. You know those are the only medicines we have. And we just had to use a bunch on one guy."

"Maybe you guys can find some more. There's a lot of you; some people can go foraging, right?"

Maya took a step closer and lifted her lantern. After scrutinizing Pallavi, she pulled the lantern away. "When you say we, how many of you are in the shelter?"

Should she tell the truth? If she lied, would it be better to say there was a lot more, or only a few more, people?

"You're thinking up a lie," Maya said. "That's not a very good way to get us to trust you."

"How will you know I'm lying?"

"Why don't you try telling me the truth and we can see."

Why did everything have to be a game with kids this age? "Me, my brother, and my dad. But my dad is real sick. That's why I had to take the medicine."

"What kind of sick? Are you a nurse?"

"I've had some training," Pallavi said.

Maya seemed to accept that lie. "So, you know how to make him better, right? You took the medicine that you needed. Why are you here again? Is your brother sick too?"

Man, this kid was good. Pallavi thought she was a good liar, but Maya saw through every one of them. "It's not working."

"How sick is he? You didn't tell me what kind of sick."

"It's not contagious, whatever it is." Pallavi surrendered her attempts at lies. Maya hadn't run away like she expected. Pallavi's dad kept drilling into them the way people treated the infected; they killed them, or they quarantined them until they died. "He has a fever, and he is coughing really badly, and he mostly sleeps. The medicine I took was an antibiotic, and that should have cured him."

CHAPTER FOURTEEN

Lena knew she had put Evan on the spot by asking him to talk. But she really needed a delaying tactic, and making him tell the story again might reveal subtle changes since his visit to the Fort. She still wasn't sure that she trusted him, but he passed their test.

The supposed envoys from Crystal were putting on a front. Lena couldn't tell whether it was because they disagreed with the offer, or maybe they were in a weaker position than they presented. Maybe they needed the alliance as much as, or more than, the farm.

"I don't know if you know who we are," Evan started.

"We've heard stories from people who passed by the Community of Hope. Or should I say escaped capture." Joseph didn't cover any of his disdain with diplomacy.

Lena was starting to see the uphill battle that Prosperity would fight until they had some allies.

"There've been a lot of changes. When was the last time you heard of us doing anything bad?"

That made Lena pay more attention. Evan wasn't just trying to explain everything away, he was drawing Moira and Joseph into it.

Moira touched Joseph's shoulder. "I'll agree it's been a while," she said, her tone less harsh. "What has changed?"

Evan told the story of Abigail's demise. "So, you can see we're in a different position. We're also seeking alliances. I've been here at the farm for a few days."

Lena took a sip of her moonshine to cover her smile. That was smart. She saw Moira and Joseph's reactions. They thought the farm and Prosperity were joining forces.

"Lena," Evan said, "do you mind if I share what I found while I was out there?"

Lena nodded, fascinated with the change in this young man. With that question, he solidified the assumption that they had an alliance. She would have to talk to the others when he wasn't around to find out how they felt about joining up with Prosperity.

"I'm going to guess that one of the reasons you want to form alliances is for defense." He waited for a response, and when they nodded, he continued. "Have you lost people recently? I mean, like disappeared loss, not accident loss or natural causes loss?"

Neither of the envoys replied.

"Do you think it's a secret?" Lena asked. "It's not like we're looking for a tactical advantage. As you pointed out there's only a few of us; even if we wanted to use it, we couldn't."

Joseph pursed his lips in denial of the logic. "Then what reason could you have for wanting to know?"

"I can give you a few," Lena said. "First of all, if you want an alliance we need to trust each other, and sharing information is part of building that trust. And we have some information, your answers might help confirm that. Do I need to come up with more?"

"I don't think they're trying to trick us, Joseph," Moira said. "Yes. Two people have disappeared in the last couple of weeks."

"I'm guessing teenage boys," Evan said.

Moira nodded. "We believe they may have run off, but we don't know where. And, if they don't want to live in Crystal, we don't intend to make them." The last was said in an accusatory tone.

"I don't think any of us would want to make someone stay, if they wanted to leave," Evan said. "But those boys are probably at the Fort now. Cole is kidnapping teens, and, I'm guessing, he's torturing them into becoming his soldiers."

"It's a bit of a stretch," Moira said. "The Fort is a long way from Crystal."

Lena tossed back the last of her moonshine and put the glass on the table with a bang. It made a good gavel. "It is, but we can hash this out later. I think it's time you told us what your conditions are."

Maya felt sorry for the girl. When she talked about her dad, her voice got all tight. And if she was right, and the pills were getting stale, it wouldn't make any difference if Pallavi had the medicine, or if they kept them.

"Why are you in a shelter?" Maya hadn't been very far from the farm, maybe there were hidden places everywhere. Little communities of people surviving by stealing from everyone.

Pallavi shrugged. "My dad thought it would be safer when the plagues came. Why do you live on a farm?"

Maya giggled. "My mom thought it would be safer than the city." She put the lantern on the floor. "I guess we're all stuck following our parents' decisions." *Maybe they need more than just medicine.* "What are you eating? Like, did your dad stock up lots of food for you? Or do you have a garden inside? How would that work?"

Pallavi drew back at that question.

"I'm not being nosy, I promise," Maya added.

"Yes, he stocked up a lot of stuff that would last, and we have a little garden that gets water from the rain, and sunlight from a glass panel in the roof."

"And you've been taking some of our food, too."

"Do I have to answer all your questions? You know I'm older than you, right?"

"If you want my help, answer my questions. You can always deal with one of the adults, if you're concerned about talking to a kid." Maya hated it when teenagers pretended they were adults. It happened all the time in New Surrey before they left. But now, everyone treated her and Jason just like they were people. Pallavi's attitude got on her nerves.

"What kind of help can you give me?" Pallavi asked, rolling her eyes.

Maya tried not to react. She knew Pallavi was scared of being turned in as the thief. But that should make her be nice, not act like Maya was a pain. "I could get some more medication for you. And some food."

That seemed to surprise Pallavi. She opened her mouth to say something, then closed it and frowned.

Maya needed to hurry this along. She wasn't due to be relieved from guard duty for an hour or so, but her mom might check on her, and that would be a disaster. "So, do you want my help?"

"No, but I need it. How come you're willing to give me this stuff?"

"I would feel really bad if something horrible happened to you." Maya knew better than to say they had excess supplies. If they got caught, she could just fudge the numbers on what she was planning to put aside for her experiments. "It's gonna take me a little while to get everything together. You should go. Just tell me where to meet you."

Pallavi looked around, as though she was making a shopping list. Then she shook her head and looked Maya in the eye. "If you're playing a game with me, kid..."

"My name is Maya, and why would I play a game with you? Where can I bring the stuff?" If Pallavi didn't answer her, then

Maya was just going to go call somebody from the house. *Why were people so difficult?*

"Okay, you know there's a stream, right?" When Maya nodded, Pallavi continued. "There's a little cave about twenty minutes' walk upstream. If you leave the stuff in the cave, I can get it without anyone seeing me."

"Okay. You should leave now. I'll make sure the delivery is in the cave just after the sun is up tomorrow."

Pallavi looked at her intensely again, and then just said "thank you", and ran to the back of the root cellar. Maya heard a faint creak as the board was pushed back into place.

Maya grabbed another empty sack, and started filling it with produce. She'd have to sneak into the house to get some meds, but if she tucked the sack of vegetables in the corner, it would be easy to grab when she was ready to go.

"Maya?"

Her mom was there. She was so intent on what she was picking for Pallavi, she hadn't heard the door open.

"What are you doing?" Her mother was staring at sack.

It had been easy to imagine that she could pretend that she was taking vegetables to test various methods of preserving them. But now that it was real, Maya remembered her mother always knew when she was lying. But she had to try. "I made a note in the book. I thought I'd try sun drying some, oven drying some more, and maybe pickling." She stopped talking before she said too much.

"Aren't those sacks over there enough for your tests?" Ava pointed to where Maya's real test supplies were.

Maya felt the blush creeping up her face, and knew she was in trouble.

CHAPTER FIFTEEN

Ava couldn't believe what she was seeing. She should have trusted her gut, even if it made her feel like she was betraying her daughter.

"I thought you would be meeting with the people from Crystal for a while." Maya blushed, clearly realizing she'd pretty much admitted to stealing.

"Lena called a break. I thought I'd come out and see if you needed anything. But clearly, you're quite capable of taking what you want."

"But Mom..."

Ava held up her hand to stop more lies coming out. "Put that stuff back. I guess we don't need to guard the stores anymore. You might as well go back to the house."

It looked for a moment like Maya was going to argue. But then she started unpacking the sack and placing the contents back where they belonged.

What could have made her daughter turn to this?

When the sack was empty, Ava pointed to the door. What Maya had already put aside for testing could stay where it was.

"Do I get to tell my side of the story?"

It broke Ava's heart to hear the pain in her daughter's voice. But right now, she couldn't listen to whatever tale Maya had made up. They were in the middle of negotiations with the envoys from Crystal. And they clearly weren't going to just sign an agreement. So everyone needed to show solidarity.

"Eventually. When we get in the house, you're to go to your room and wait till I come talk to you. You'll go up the stairs quietly." Maya was walking slumped just ahead of her. Ava touched her shoulder to get her attention. "Do you understand what I'm saying?"

Maya swallowed and wiped at her nose. "You don't want me to make a scene."

The timing was so wrong, but a screaming argument might be just what they needed. "That's right. I want to know everything from you before I take it to Lena, or anyone else. When the meeting's over, I'll come talk to you."

Maya sniffed. Ava could see dampness at the corners of her eyes.

"So, you are going to listen to me?"

If it was just the two of them, Ava would have grounded her daughter, and taken her word that she wouldn't do it again. But it wasn't. Somehow, she would have to prepare Maya for what the group might do. "I'll listen, but you better not lie to me."

They entered through the kitchen door. Ava turned Maya toward her. Taking a damp cloth from the sink, she washed the evidence of tears off her cheeks. "When you walk through that room, you smile, say goodnight, and then go up to your room."

Maya grimaced.

"I said smile."

Maya made an effort, and it was a smile, a sad one, but it would pass.

The meeting was coming back to order as they passed through. Ava introduced her daughter to the envoys, Maya said goodnight, and went upstairs.

. . .

Lena watched Maya move past everyone who was sitting at the table. The girl was subdued, which was very unusual. She couldn't think about that now; there was no more delaying whatever the deal was from these two people. Lena couldn't stop fretting that this might be the end of their community.

"Okay, we're ready," she said. This time there were no refreshments on the table, which was a good thing. Getting a little too relaxed on the moonshine would probably not be sensible.

Moira took three sheets of paper from the bag on the floor beside her. They were stapled, and it looked like there was only one copy. "As I mentioned, we are concerned about losing our autonomy by agreeing too quickly." She flipped to the second page and placed her finger halfway down. Lena could see there was a list. "First thing is we need to agree on an exit strategy." She looked around the table. "I'm sure none of us wants to face a fight to get out of an agreement that isn't working."

Lena was thankful that everybody kept their faces impassive.

When no one reacted, Moira continued. "The second point is, each community will appoint one liaison officer, and that person will have full authority to make decisions." She looked around again.

"Just read them all out," Lena said. "There's no benefit in doling them out piece by piece."

"Fine, there are only three other points. Nobody makes new alliances or ends one without everybody agreeing. So, if you want to end the alliance with Prosperity, do it now or you'll need our say so. If this works, and we have more partners, you'll need a majority of the allies to agree."

"I'm assuming you're making this a standard," Lena said. "By 'you' you mean 'a community', right?"

"Yes. I'll keep going, shall I?" Moira asked. "All resources will be made available as needed and as required. The final point: representation on a joint Council will be based on population."

Lena was glad it wasn't her choice. There was something wrong with this deal, and if it was up to her she would say no and move on. It wasn't just up to her though, and when they discussed it as a group she wanted everyone clear on what was being proposed. "How long do we have before we need to give you an answer?"

"If what that young man has told us is true about Cole's activities," Joseph said. "Then I wouldn't take too long. Shall we say three days?"

"We have some questions." Lena looked around the table and saw nods. "I'll start. You say the council will be proportionately represented? Given that we are so few, I need to know what that means to us."

Moira smiled. She'd been anticipating this question, Lena could tell. "It is intended to give you a measure of power. It would be proportional based on the ratio between our population and yours. I don't know the actual calculation, but it would be something like if you had three people on the council, we would have no more than four."

Still a majority

Lena nodded for Jason to ask his question.

"I don't understand the difference between developing an exit strategy and having the rule about if you want to leave you have to have approval."

Joseph pushed his glasses up his nose. "Good question, young man. The first point is intended to design how we would untangle our alliance, should one of us wish to leave. The approval point is intended to ensure that there is some, shall we say, life to the alliance. It would certainly be of no benefit, should anyone wish to make an alliance and then simply pull out a few weeks later. In fact, it would be dangerous to do business that way. Someone would simply form an alliance to get what they needed. And then step away."

"Yeah, I suppose that makes sense," Jason said.

"And what about that part about all resources will be made available?" Tik asked.

"That will be something we can negotiate," Moira said. "I'm sure you can appreciate that we didn't prepare for every possible scenario. Perhaps a little trust would go a long way here."

CHAPTER SIXTEEN

Ava wasn't feeling very trustful. And, as much as she tried to separate the Maya situation from this negotiation, she couldn't.

"I think we have enough, Lena," Ava said. "It's late. Joseph, Moira, why don't we settle you in for the night." She stood ready to show them to the room they'd prepared. This time it was Mellow who would be sleeping on the couch, although she'd probably end up in Tik's temporary bed.

Moira looked at Lena, as though surprised that someone else had brought the meeting to a close.

"Good idea," Lena said. She stood and gestured toward the staircase. "We'll all do better for a night's rest."

Ava watched both envoys stand. They weren't preparing to go upstairs.

"If the negotiation is truly over," Moira said. "Then Joseph and I will be on our way. You can send a representative after us to deliver your decision."

Everyone reacted as if they had proposed walking naked through a blackberry bush.

Keith was the first to speak. "That's very dangerous. If you will wait a few hours, I can escort you part of the way when the sun comes up."

"We are perfectly capable of defending ourselves against whatever comes at us at night." Joseph took Moira's arm and they headed for the front door.

"Didn't you hear what I reported?" Evan said. "You might run into something more than just a wild animal."

"We heard you," Joseph said. "Nevertheless, we will be leaving."

Ava waited for someone to talk them into staying. It felt wrong to let them go, no matter what they assured about their defense. But no one spoke. Within minutes the two were on their way.

"Someone should follow," Evan said, standing. "If something happens to those envoys, no matter what you agree to, that town is going to be suspicious."

"I agree, it seems crazy," Lena said. "But they got here without an escort. And they seemed very confident that they were going to be okay. Maybe they have an armed escort waiting for them just out of sight."

Ava had nothing to add. There was no wrong side of that argument. It was dangerous, and they were determined to go. It was time for Ava to confront her daughter.

At the top of the stairs Ava stood in front of Maya's door. There was no sound from inside, although she didn't know what she was expecting to hear. She knocked, and Maya said to come in.

"Are you ready to tell me the truth?" Ava asked.

"Would you believe anything I say? Maybe I already told you the truth."

She couldn't believe her daughter was stealing for no reason. But all Maya's behavior screamed that she was lying. "Okay, if that's where you want to start. You're grounded for three days." Her years of teaching experience had taught Ava a lot of things.

The most important lesson had been not to underestimate the stubbornness of a preteen. They weren't quite as emotional as a teenager, but they knew their mind and the only way to persuade them to look at another point of view was to treat them as if they knew what they were doing.

"So that's it? You're going to punish me without listening?" Maya's cheeks were blazing.

"I know I said we had more vegetables than we can eat. It's not so much that we'll miss them, but the fact that you felt you could just take them. I know you; you're not greedy. You must've had a good reason. But don't try to tell me it was for experiments." Ava hoped that her daughter would be such an easy read for the rest of their lives, but knew it wouldn't happen. Eventually Maya would learn to keep her secrets. But now, everything she was thinking played on her face. "Don't try to make something up. I'll know if you're lying."

Maya turned her back on her mother and stared out the window. She probably didn't realize that Ava could see her reflection. The frown left her daughter's face a split second before she turned.

"You're right, I did have enough for my experiments. And I'm pretty sure we'll be able to put aside enough food to trade with. That's what we need, right? As you guys form alliances, you'll need something to trade with. And we need traveling food. You can't really take a bag of apples with you on a trip if you're going to be gone for a week or two. Because that will eventually happen, we'll start farther away. We'll have to go scavenging."

Ava nodded, knowing that if she responded aloud, Maya would keep moving down that track instead of answering the actual question. Now Maya picked at the bedspread, threads of chenille spreading around the bald patch she was creating.

"I was going to use it to try to lure in some of the rabbits and other animals that live in the woods." She looked from the bedspread to Ava.

They were getting closer to the truth, Ava knew as Maya worked on her second lie. But that look meant that Maya was checking to see if Ava was buying it. So, this wasn't the final story. "Go on."

"I thought maybe if we could kind of domesticate them, then we wouldn't have to hunt so much."

That sounded more like her daughter, planning ahead rather than waiting until something was needed. Ava was still convinced that there was more to the story. But it was going to take a long time to wear her daughter down.

"You're still grounded," Ava said. "In the future, don't just go off on your own ideas."

"How long am I grounded for?"

"Until you convince me that you aren't holding something back."

"What are you going to tell everyone?" Maya asked, keeping her gaze on the bed.

"I won't tell them anything. At least this time. Don't put me in this position again."

Maya nodded.

Ava left the room and joined the others downstairs. The moonshine was out, the discussion was heated, and two members were missing.

Lena held up a glass for Ava. "We're waiting for Scott and Keith to come back. They're just making sure our guests are well on their way."

Maya could hear the conversations going on downstairs from her room. Not the exact words, just the noise. Every once in a while it sounded like people were yelling, but mostly it was calm. They rarely fought at the farm, at least not over important things. Her mom had been gone for a while and Maya was getting really worried about how much time had passed. Pallavi would be waiting for her soon, and Maya didn't even have the food she needed.

She could get the medication and then sneak out. She'd leave a note for Pallavi to say that she would try to get vegetables the next day. Maya couldn't let her down.

Her mom's room was just at the end of the hall so Maya carefully opened her door only about a quarter of the way; it would creak if she went any farther. She slipped through, just as the voices were raised again downstairs. First she had to see what was going on, so she wouldn't get surprised if they were almost finished the discussion.

She sat on the top step. She could hear everything clearly, and no one could see her.

By now everyone was a little drunk. And Maya had no idea what those people from Crystal had said at the table, but it must've been something bad.

"We can't just say yes, or no," Deb said. "We don't have enough power to say no, and if we say yes we never will."

Maya could remember when everybody hated Deb because she was such a spoilt brat for someone her mom's age. But she was a really good nurse, and she understood these negotiations really well. Maya wondered for a second if she should bring Deb along to the cave. They could wait for Pallavi and then convince her to let them check out her father. Of course, that would mean explaining that she was actually lying to her mom, and she was stealing supplies.

She was getting ready to sneak to her mom's room, when Evan said something. Why was he allowed to join the discussion? He wasn't one of them. She settled back on the step.

"But we offer you what you need," Evan said. "You need numbers, Prosperity has numbers. Even if we agree to negotiate, it will look like you have more allies. I'm not saying you need to sign your lives away."

"You know, that's not a bad idea," her mom said. "Not

agreeing to anything with Prosperity," she added over objections that people started shouting. "I meant Redstone. We could open negotiations with Redstone."

"We won't meet Crystal's deadline," Jason said. "Don't we have to give them an answer in three days? That means we have to decide and start out tomorrow."

"We don't just have to accept what they tell us," Lena said. "Tomorrow we'll just have somebody go catch up with those envoys. Just tell them we need a week. Anyone have any objections to Ava's idea?"

Maya felt proud of her mom. Since nobody objected, it meant they all agreed that she had a good idea.

"Okay, we'll figure out who's all going," Lena said, her voice a little slurry. "But I think Evan should be part of that team. He explains Prosperity's position well. And you'll make sure they understand that maybe we are going to make an alliance with you."

The conversation changed. They were no longer discussing anything, which meant people would start coming up to bed. Maya knew she wouldn't be able to sneak out of the house, but she might have time to get the meds from her mom's room.

She crept down the hall, and pushed her mom's bedroom door open.

The box of medications was kept under the bed. Maya had been there when they had them. She lay on the floor and slid her hand underneath the bed. And there was nothing there. Someone had moved them.

CHAPTER SEVENTEEN

Maya stood outside the little cave where she was supposed to leave the medicine. The good thing about the grown-ups drinking so much last night was they were all sound asleep as soon as they went to bed. She didn't dare go searching for the medication, but she'd been able to sneak out of the house and grabbed a sack of food. She didn't care anymore what her mom thought. Although, to be truthful, she realized that she would care very much when she had to face her.

Getting across the field had been hard in the dark, but she had been too afraid to light the lantern until she was well away from the house. She'd skinned her knee, but she hoped it would be worth it.

Maya thought through her two plans; now that she was here, her optimism was replaced by lots of questions. Whatever happened, she wasn't going to leave Pallavi and her family alone with their problems.

The best thing would be if she could see the dad. Then she could try to convince them to let Deb check him out. That was plan A, but she wasn't sure Pallavi would go for it.

Her second plan was to explain to Pallavi what was happening and promise that she would bring medications as soon as she could. They couldn't be running out of pills already, she must have some time to get them.

But it all depended on Pallavi showing up. Maya hoped that would happen soon. The longer she was gone, the more likely they'd come looking for her. Probably not here, but eventually, she would have to give up and go home and face the punishment that was coming her way.

If it wasn't for the worry about everyone, this would be a good place to hang out. Maya held up the lantern to look at the entrance to the cave. It stood about a foot above where the river ran, so should always stay dry — unless there was some kind of freak storm — and it would be cool here in the heat of summer.

The lantern didn't shine very far into the cave. It was hard to trust Pallavi's promise that there would be no animals inside, and that it was a safe place to leave supplies. Maybe, when the sun came up, if she was still here, she'd feel better about going in, but right now Maya was willing to sit outside on a rock with the sack at her side.

There was a breeze here. It kept the insects away, but sucked the warmth out of Maya's body. She wrapped her arms around herself and tried to ignore the little pops, cracks, and rustling sounds around her.

Maya jerked awake at the sound of the dawn chorus of birds.

The sack was still beside her, thank goodness.

Pallavi wasn't there and now Maya was getting hungry. Someone at the farm would be getting up to make breakfast right about now. A raw carrot or radish didn't sound as appetizing as bacon and eggs.

Maya remembered how she'd felt when Deb butchered two of the pigs. In her mind, she knew that the animals on the farm were going to be food eventually, but it hadn't really sunk in until that happened. She'd tried to be a vegetarian, and that had lasted until someone cooked the meat. Suddenly it was just food, not her pets.

"You were supposed to leave the stuff here."

No amount of moonshine enabled Evan to forget what happened last night. Were they insane? Sending him off to help negotiate an agreement with another town — when he had no official standing.

This morning his mouth felt like someone had painted ashes all over it while he'd slept. He could smell breakfast; someone was frying bacon. A strong cup of tea and a greasy breakfast would go a long way to curing his hangover.

When he got downstairs it was apparent last night's discussion had been continued in his absence. Lena pointed him to a chair and poured him tea.

"You'll be leaving soon." Lena took a plate and started filling it with food.

Evan wasn't sure how they'd arranged everything so quickly, but he knew there was no point in arguing with them. He broke the yolk of the egg on his plate with the corner of his toast and started eating. They would tell him what they wanted him to do without him expending energy asking.

"Keith went after the envoys from Crystal already," Lena said. "Deb's packing you some ointment; you'll need to keep that hand clean, so it will heal. Scott's going with you; he's packing up your supplies right now."

Evan swallowed his mouthful of food. "So, what exactly are you expecting to happen?"

Lena sat down beside him and poured herself a mug of tea. "We need some strength. The alliances are going to be a good thing, I really believe that. The problem is, until we have some people on our side, we don't stand a chance in making an equitable agreement."

"Prosperity would do that with you," Evan said.

"You're going to be working at building the trust we need for that agreement," Lena said.

"You know, we're in kind of the same position as you are. You don't have enough people, and we don't have anyone's trust. You should just sign up with us."

Lena shook her head. "Maybe after this. Scott will speak for us at Redstone. Your job is to get them to understand the value."

"What you mean is," Evan said, wondering how far he could push Lena. "You want me to be the muscle. If they don't jump on board after Scott's done his thing, I make sure they realize that Prosperity is going to jump all over them. So, the last thing you want is for me to come across all reasonable."

Lena laughed. "Let's hope it won't come to that. Hopefully they'll see that we're all making alliances and they're being invited in, not threatened to join."

Evan was relieved. Prosperity would never change their image if these people were just going to use them as a threat. "Okay. We won't have much time when we're there, but we'll do our best."

His plate was clear, and Evan stood to help do the chores.

"We'll take care of that," Ava said, taking his plate from his hand. "Go see Deb, and then get your horse ready."

"We should probably ride a little faster now that we're on the flats," Evan said. They were about two hours out from the farm, and Scott didn't seem to understand how far they had to go.

"This stretch doesn't run that far," Scott said. "We won't make up much time. In fact, we'll lose time if one of the horses gets hurt."

"It felt weird leaving when everyone started the search for Maya," Evan said. It was only minutes before they'd set out that Ava checked on Maya. No one knew how long the girl had been gone. "Do you think she'll be okay?"

Scott nudged his horse a little closer. "Maya knows how to take care of herself. You don't know them well enough to notice, but Ava and Maya had a fight last night. Maya has probably just gone somewhere to cool off. Maybe punish her mom a bit. But we've trained both those kids to look after themselves." He laughed. "Well, how to take care of themselves in the countryside, not how to take care themselves when faced with a mother's wrath."

"I'm pretty sure that's a lesson we all learn through experience." Evan was trying to figure out how to bring up the subject of Prosperity. He had to find a way to get them to believe things were very different. If this thing with Redstone didn't work out, he'd have to go home. In fact, he wouldn't be going back to the farm unless there was hope for the alliance.

"I guess I'll find out when we have kids. Lena's coming around to the idea," Scott said. "Although that might have more to do with the fact that we're running out of birth control, than an actual choice."

"Yes. The world is changing in little tiny ways every day. You think you've accepted how things will work, then something stupid, like condoms, runs out."

"Or, you go along living your life and then one day some asshole decides to start taking over your little world." Scott rolled his shoulders, and patted his rifle. "We should be sitting around, enjoying this time. Harvesting a little during the day, and relaxing in the evening. Maybe when we got Newton Cole sorted out, that's what will happen."

That was Evan's opening. "The only way that we're going to be able to sort him out is to stop him. And to do that we need to get these alliances done. And maybe we'll have to all put the past behind us, and start fresh."

Scott chuckled. He scanned the hills around them as he rode. They both spent more time looking around than they did looking ahead.

"You're asking a lot," Scott said. "Putting the past behind us, and starting fresh. There's two ways that can work out. The one that you think, that we all end up working together and no one gets hurt. And then there's the other one; we all learn that nobody changes that much."

Ever since he'd been sent out to meet with these people, Evan had been wishing that someone else had been on duty that day when they passed through. In fact, he wished he'd had a job that kept him out of the public eye. It would be so much easier to convince people that Prosperity wasn't trying to steal from them if he didn't carry his own guilt from being part of it.

"So, how am I supposed to do this?"

"Convince us you can be trusted? I don't know, half of us are ready to believe you just because they're scared. I haven't made up my mind, but it's not up to me."

They should have sent someone more persuasive.

"Let's hope I figure out how to deal with it before Newton Cole takes over."

Scott flicked the reins, and his horse began to canter. "This is where we speed up."

CHAPTER EIGHTEEN

"You shouldn't have come," Pallavi said. "You said you would leave the stuff here, why did you come?"

How could she have been so stupid as to trust this kid? She was probably snooping around just for something to do.

"It didn't go quite as I expected," Maya said. She patted a sack beside her.

Something in the way Maya looked down at the water told Pallavi there were no pills in the sack. "What happened?"

"I thought you'd be here earlier. I thought..." Maya sighed and looked up at Pallavi. "I couldn't get the medication. It's been moved, and I have to hunt for it. My mom thinks I'm stealing, and now I've been away almost all day. No one is going to trust me. You should let our nurse see your dad." The words burst forth without a breath.

Pallavi felt sorry for Maya. She was going to be in trouble when she got home. But her dad wouldn't let a stranger in. Even in his fever, he would know that this nurse didn't belong. Then he'd start worrying and that would make him sicker.

"Tell your mom that you had to be alone to think things

through. When she sees you, she'll probably be more relieved than mad." Pallavi reached for the sack.

"You don't know my mom," Maya said. She pushed the supplies closer to Pallavi. "What about the nurse? If I can tell them the truth, they will want to help."

"No. I can't let anyone know where we are. It's too dangerous."

"Do you know there are raiding parties?" Maya looked around like someone was about to jump out from behind a rock. "I overheard something about the Fort capturing kids to fight for them."

When her dad heard that, they would never convince him to leave. "So? They don't know where my family is."

Maya stood and then stepped down to join Pallavi. "You are alone out here. Me too. If they get you, they won't go looking for your family. They'll have you."

Maya stared at Pallavi.

She can't know what that really means. "Same goes for you," Pallavi said. She wanted to run back to the shelter. No matter what she said to Maya, the news had her jumpy. As soon as she knew Maya was on her way back to the farm, Pallavi was heading back. Mahir needed to know what was going on.

"I'm fast and I can hide."

Pallavi resisted the urge to argue. Maya needed to go home.

"Okay, I guess you know what you're doing. I'll watch from here until you're out of sight." Pallavi wasn't sure she would stay, but Maya wouldn't know.

"I should come with you," Maya said. "I won't tell anyone where you are if you don't want me to."

Not a chance.

If Maya couldn't get the pills, Pallavi would have to hope the rest of the dose she had would be enough. If she could get another series, it would be better. "No. I need to get back. If you can't get me medicine, I'll go looking other places." She lifted the sack over her shoulder. "Go home."

Maya looked like she was about to cry, but then she straightened her shoulders. "I can try for more of the pills. But if I can't get them, you still need food. If you came to the farm, we would give you more than that." She pointed to the stolen supplies.

"We don't need the food. We need medicine."

Does she think I'm stupid?

Maya battled with herself. She knew the best thing would be for Pallavi to give in and let her go see her dad. But she also knew she couldn't hang around arguing all day. No matter how glad her mom would be to see her, Maya was in a boatload of trouble. She couldn't just leave it there though. She would feel awful if something happened to Pallavi, like it was her fault.

"They've hidden away the box of medicine," Maya said. "It's gonna take me a while to figure a way to search for it, and then how to take it out of the house."

Pallavi stared at her, and Maya wondered if she was just going to be stubborn enough to outlast Maya's patience. Then she gave her head a little shake. "It's too dangerous for you to be running back and forth from the farm to here."

"If we are careful, it should be okay." Maya wasn't going to let Pallavi refuse her help. Sure, it was going to be dangerous, but her mom would not have let the medicines get too far away. Maya didn't think she would have to search every room. They were probably with Deb, or Lena. "We also have books. I can look up what's wrong with your dad if you tell me his symptoms."

"Why are you trying so hard to help me?"

Maya hoped the question meant that Pallavi was going to give in. "Because I know who you are. I mean, I don't really know who you are. I just mean you're not some faceless person. I know something about you. If I didn't help, and we found your family dead someday, I would feel like it's my fault." As the words came out, Maya realized that it wasn't quite the truth. "I mean I would help anybody; I really do want to help you. I just can't worry about people I don't know. We have enough food to spare. At least, until we join up with the other towns, then maybe we won't, without more people working the land. And Deb, our nurse, said maybe the meds won't work after a while. So, if you need them, at least they won't go to waste." That was the most she'd spoken to a stranger since they left New Surrey.

Pallavi was getting nervous, Maya noticed that she kept looking around. Maya couldn't hear any threats. Apparently Pallavi couldn't either, because she relaxed.

"Maybe that's why they're not working on Dad." She stepped closer. "He has a fever that won't break. And he doesn't seem to be able to stay awake. When I feed him, or he takes his pills, it's like he's doing it without really understanding what's going on. It's lasted more than a week. I'm giving him more than the dose that it said in the book. He should be getting better by now. And he's not."

Maya regretted promising not to tell anyone. If she could give Deb that whole description, she would bet a month's chores that Deb would figure it out and cure Pallavi's dad. "Okay, the soonest I'll be able to get out again is really early in the morning. I'm probably going to be totally grounded, so sneaking out will take some time. But I'll be back here before the sun is up, and I'll have a whole bottle of the medicines." No matter how hard it was going to be, Maya knew that she would make that promise true.

"Okay," Pallavi said, reaching to give Maya a hug. "I'll be here as early as I can."

Maya pulled away from the hug. She didn't say anything, just started running for home.

CHAPTER NINETEEN

Boy, had her mom been mad. Apparently, they'd been searching for her all day. Pallavi was right, her mom was definitely more relieved than angry, at least at first. Maya was surprised to find out they were all kind of on her side when her mom got over her fear enough to start yelling. It still meant she was assigned a ton of chores. She had to rush to do them before dinner because she'd gotten home so late, and then had to go to her room after dinner. None of that got in the way of her plans.

If her mom had known she wanted to search everyone's room, Maya was pretty sure that she wouldn't have been assigned to clean everyone's room. She'd managed to keep a pout on her face when she learned about the task.

The pills had been in Deb's room. There was no lock on the box, and it was just sitting under the bed. It had been too risky to take them then; if Deb went looking and Maya was still around, her mom would know exactly what happened.

Now it was after dinner, and she was supposed to be in her room. But everybody was downstairs again, arguing over what Crystal had wanted and how they felt about it. It meant she could probably take what she needed, and slip away before anyone noticed.

Maya slipped open her door just wide enough to be able to hear what was going on around her. There was a lot of talking downstairs. She had to believe they were all downstairs.

This was the easy part; if she was caught in the hallway, she would just say she was going to the bathroom. She could use the same excuse after she had the meds. The only time it would be a problem was exactly when she was going into Deb's room. She hadn't been able to come up with an excuse that sounded believable in her ears.

As soon as she had what she needed, Maya would sneak out her bedroom window, after picking up the lantern and a kitchen knife she'd taken earlier. She wasn't going to be caught and taken by the guys at the Fort easily if they found her.

She knew where every squeaky board was in the hall between bedrooms, so Maya carefully made her way to Deb's room. She turned the handle on the door, and realized that it would all be different after they learned what she'd done. It was probably the end of not locking your door at the farm.

She couldn't think about that.

The door opened quietly, thanks to the little bit of grease she'd rubbed into the hinge when she cleaned it.

Before she went in, she listened carefully, but there seemed to be no change to the noise downstairs. She closed the door behind her and tiptoed to the side of the bed, bending and reaching for the box as soon as she arrived there. When she opened the lid, nothing had changed. She took that as a good sign, nobody suspected anything. She slid one of the bottles into her pocket after opening it and filling the gap with one of her socks. She couldn't afford to have the bottle rattle and give her away. Before she closed the lid, Maya checked to see what else was in there that Pallavi's family might need. She added a few Band-Aids and alcohol wipes to her pocket. She slid the box back under the bed, checking to make sure it was in exactly the same position. When she got to Deb's bedroom door, Maya realized she hadn't counted on the fact that she'd have to open the door without knowing who was outside in the hallway. Now her heart started beating real fast. And she couldn't catch her breath.

Get hold of yourself. You can't stay in here all night, and the longer you wait, the more likely someone is going to be out there.

She leaned against the door and held her breath. She couldn't hear anything, but that didn't make her feel any better as she turned the handle and cracked the door open. If someone was watching, they would know she was there. She peeked out and no one was there, so she slipped out of Deb's room, and pushed the door until she heard a click.

"What are you doing in my room?"

Keith stepped out of the bathroom as the door shut. There was no way Maya could get away with denying being in the room. While she was planning, she'd always thought of it as Deb's room, but it was Keith's room too.

He took a step toward her. "Maya, what were you doing in the room?"

Maya could see he was more concerned than angry, but if she couldn't come up with a reasonable explanation, she would never get out of the house tonight. "I had a headache." It was all she could think of under pressure. "I thought there was some aspirin."

"I don't think so," he said. "But Deb made some of that willow bark tea. It works the same. I'll go get you some."

"No, that's okay," she blurted. "I probably just need a nap." She watched Keith think it over. Of all the people to run into up here, it had to be the one who taught her how to hunt. Keith could read the tiniest details. Would he see the lie on her face? "Don't tell my mom; she'll only worry." *Stop talking, you're just making him more suspicious.*

"I'll check on you in a while. If it gets worse, we'll see about that tea." He watched her as she returned to her room.

When Maya closed the door behind her, her knees went weak. There was no guarantee that Keith had believed her, but he hadn't pushed, so that was a victory. Unfortunately, not a complete win; now she couldn't sneak out in case someone checked on her before she could get far enough away.

Pallavi sat on a rock outside the cave; the sun was up, and had been for a while. She felt stupid for trusting Maya. The kid talked like an adult, but she really was only Mahir's age. And that meant she made promises that she couldn't keep.

The only thing she learned that was any use was that the medication wasn't going to be available to steal. Pallavi might be able to sneak into a root cellar, but into the house? That was a whole world of risks. She didn't want to think about what it meant for her dad, that she couldn't get more pills.

"You come here just to sit in the sun?" Mahir asked.

Pallavi couldn't quite get the breath to answer him. How had she become so inattentive as to let her brother sneak up on her? What if it had been somebody from the Fort?

"I didn't mean to scare you," Mahir said. "I just couldn't sit with Dad anymore. Maybe we can do some fishing."

As much as she wanted to, Pallavi couldn't make an argument to Mahir. Staying with her dad was hard because his breathing was getting worse and now he cried out in his sleep; it was scary, not just heartbreaking. "Did you bring something to fish with?"

"I can make a spear." Mahir started picking through some smaller branches. "I have my knife. I can make a point on something like this."

He sounded confident, but Pallavi was reminded that Maya had sounded confident too. Keeping that news from him felt bad now. If their dad got worse, they would need to work as a team. So keeping secrets was dangerous. "I came here to meet someone." She told him about Maya and the pills.

Mahir nodded. "I guess it makes sense, or it did when you made the deal, right?" He sat beside her on the rock. "How old is she?"

"About your age." Pallavi winced at the confession.

"Would you have made that deal with me?" Mahir sounded hurt.

"I shouldn't have made it with her. But I don't know her very well, and that made me forget how young she was. So, no, I would not have made the deal with you. And I should not have made it with her. I put Maya in a bad position. Who knows what's happened."

"We should go see if she needs help."

In any other circumstances, Pallavi would have agreed. But this world was so different. They couldn't worry more about someone else than themselves. It bothered her to think that way, but it was how things were. "We should be trying to figure out where we can get more medicine. Even if we did go to the farm, how could we help her?"

Mahir looked at her as if she were crazy. "She might not be there. She might be hurt somewhere on her way. If she is at home, we could maybe tell the truth. How do you know they won't help us voluntarily?"

Because I'm not sure we would in the same circumstances. Pallavi knew she couldn't say that to her brother. "That's a last resort. We have to figure this out on our own. We have to be able to take care of ourselves."

"But that shouldn't mean we don't care about anyone else."

Pallavi closed her eyes. She really didn't have the energy to convince her brother that she was right. But she couldn't just let it end there. If she did, Mahir would probably end up heading to the farm by himself. "They're in a better position than we are. We can go there if it doesn't get better, but we still have a couple of days' worth of medicine for him."

Mahir stood up and walked to the edge of the river. He peered into the water. "We're not going to catch any fish today," he said. "Are you going to sit waiting for her? Are you going to come home?"

Going home won't help anyone, Pallavi thought. "You go. I'll wait a little while longer in case she comes."

CHAPTER TWENTY

Maya sat on the chair trying not to cry. Tears would just make it harder for her to explain if she had to. She hadn't slept much last night, but there had been no way for her to escape. Her mother had checked on her a little while after Keith had left which meant he'd told her. Adults couldn't be trusted.

Then, this morning when it was super quiet, she'd tried to sneak out. Lena had caught her. And they'd found the pills on her. Maya hadn't spoken a word since. Because she couldn't be sure that she wouldn't just start bawling if she tried to say something.

Lena had sent everyone away including Maya's mom, and now she sat across from Maya at the kitchen table.

"None of us really understand what's going on with you, Maya," Lena said. "If you could just tell us why, maybe we could understand. If you're sick you really need to tell us, so Deb can make it better."

It felt like they'd been doing this all morning, but Maya figured it could only have been about half an hour. She wasn't really sick. Her stomach hurt because she'd been caught, not because she had any kind of disease. And she couldn't bear to face

Deb even if she was sick, because she felt like she had stolen directly from her.

"Is someone making you do this?" Lena stood and filled the kettle with water and put it on the stove. She added some wood to the compartment, so the water would boil. "If you don't tell us, the only thing we can do is punish you. That just doesn't seem fair. But I can't just let it go, Maya. We must control our supplies. We have a lot, but you never know what could happen to make us need everything we stored up." Lena stood at the stove waiting for the kettle to boil.

What if she did tell them? Pallavi didn't know them as well as Maya did. But she promised Pallavi that she wouldn't tell, and she was going to keep that promise. She fixed her stare on the window, focusing on the distance. Maya realized that she hoped to see Pallavi crossing the field, coming to take the problem out of her hands.

Eventually the kettle boiled, and Lena poured the hot water over the teabags. Maya watched it all out of the corner of her eye.

"Maya, what else have you taken?"

Maya resisted the urge to say that she'd taken nothing. Afraid to let even the first few words out of her mouth in case the whole story tumbled after.

Lena blew on the surface of the tea to cool it, then crossed to sit in front of Maya, cutting off her ability to stare into the distance. Then she sighed. "I've known you all your life. Do you know why I'm the one asking you these questions?" When it was clear Maya was remaining silent, Lena continued. "Your mom is so mad at you right now that I don't think she would listen. And I was hoping that you would tell me the story. Because I believe there's a story, Maya. You wouldn't just steal things. You were taking them to someone, or somewhere."

Maya looked down at her hands. There was no way. If she didn't make eye contact, she could keep her mouth closed.

"Okay, I guess I don't have as much patience as you. There's only so many ways we can punish you, so you're grounded. And because everybody knows why you're grounded, no one will help you get out. If you need to go to the bathroom, call for someone. We'll bring you your food. You won't have any chores while you're grounded, but you will have to catch up when we finally find out what's going on."

"Has anybody asked why Maya's in her room?" Lena asked, keeping her eye on the carrot she was chopping. "I mean, why is she still in her room, I guess."

"I know they want to ask, but everybody is being very respectful of the fact that she's my daughter. I'm not sure how long that will last. They'll want to know why she did it eventually." Ava rinsed the potatoes in the bowl. "I don't know why she's being so stubborn. She must've had a very good reason for taking a sack of food, and trying to take our medication. I don't know why she won't just tell us."

Lena tossed the vegetables into the boiling water. "I know. Part of me is glad that we have to deal with this now, when we know everybody. As these alliances start forming, and they will, we'll be dealing with people we don't know. Something like this happens, it could threaten everything."

"So, Maya is going to be the precedent upon which we set every single punishment?" Ava started laughing. "The Maya law," she said through the chuckles.

"What a thing to be memorialized for." Lena started preparing the fish they caught today. "We have to find out what's going on. It means everyone needs to know, and everyone needs to weigh in. Are you going to be okay with that?"

Ava wouldn't meet her eyes. Lena steeled herself to argue for what she was planning. Then Ava looked up; there was sadness in her eyes, and in the smile she pasted on.

"No. But I think I'll have to get used to not being good with things when it comes to my kids. I wish there were other parents here, with other kids to act up; maybe that'll come with the alliances. Or with time; we're going run out of birth control soon."

"I want you to tell everybody what's going on," Lena said. "It'll be better that way. Everyone will know that you're on side, and still support you, rather than fight you."

Ava nodded and started dicing the potatoes. "I know you have a plan, but first let me give you my two cents. Maya can be very stubborn. We're going to need to escalate the punishment. She will eventually tell us, but we might have to drag it out of her."

"What you mean by escalating the punishment?"

"I mean, make her feel more isolated. I hate to do it; it's not the way I've raised her up to now. But she's changed the game on us. We'll tell everybody at dinner what's going on. I guess I'm happy to do it. And then we need to set guards. She needs to know that she can't just wiggle her way out of this."

Lena's only experience with preteens was from her days as a teacher. Ava's willingness to push Maya hard impressed her, and worried her. As much as Ava was going to be okay with talking about it as a plan — and, in fact, came up with it on her own — when it came down to it, she was going to have to watch her child suffer. And Lena didn't want to do that to her friend. This world had some very shitty aspects to it.

"So, someone outside her door on a permanent basis," Lena asked. "At least someone will be there when she needs to call out for something."

"Not just outside," Ava said. "Someone in her room. It will be too easy for her to slip out the window if someone's not watching her. That part will fall to you and me, and maybe Mellow. I guess Jason could help out too."

Lena put the cast-iron pan on the hottest element, and added some oil. "Okay, let's hope it doesn't take her a long time to come to her senses. We have some jobs that can be done while standing guard, but not that many. We'll need everyone in the field for last harvest soon."

Maya couldn't sleep when someone was watching her. It had been going on since before dinner, and now it wasn't that long till sunrise. It was hard not to talk because she felt like it was rude to sit quietly in her room when she wasn't alone. While it was light outside, she managed to read a book. But in the dark, she wouldn't waste a candle to read. Mellow had been with her for a while, she seemed quite willing to sit in the chair and wait.

"Would it help if I look at something else?" Mellow asked.

Maya shook her head. She was about to say it was okay when her bedroom door opened. Thank goodness for the light that came in through the window from the moon. It would have been really scary to find that someone else was in the room when they made a noise. The newcomer was her brother.

"I'll take over now," Jason said. "Mom said I was supposed to be watching until daylight. I couldn't sleep, so I came early."

Mellow stood, and patted Jason on the shoulder as she walked by. "Try to get her to sleep, it's not good for her to worry away the night."

Jason mumbled something and then took the seat that Mellow had just left. When they were alone, he shuffled the chair closer to the bed. "Okay, it's just you and me. You can tell me what's going on. I'll keep your secret, maybe I'll even help."

Maya wanted to open up to her brother, but she couldn't trust him. Not that he would betray her on purpose, but he wasn't very good at keeping secrets. After so much silence, despite her worries, she had to talk to someone. "It's best for me to keep it a secret." Just the sound of her voice made Maya feel better. It also loosened the lump that had been building in her throat since Deb had shown up on the first watch.

"You stole things we need. I can't believe you would do that. Just tell me why."

"Jason, I can't tell you because it's not my secret."

He got up off the chair and sat beside her on the bed. "Don't talk so loud. Keith is in the hall outside. He's mending ropes, but still paying attention. They're not taking any chances that you'll try to run away. Please don't do that, you're my sister and I kind of need you around. Even though you are a pest." He punched her shoulder gently.

"I would never do that. I'm part of this family. I know we talked about wanting a friend," she said. Maya closed her lips. Was that why she helped Pallavi? So she could have a friend. "But I would never go looking for one on my own."

"You were gone a long time. I was afraid that you had run away. You just need to tell us what's going on, Maya."

Jason might be two years older than her, Maya thought, but sometimes he acted like she was the older sister. "You don't need to worry so much about me; you know I can take care of myself. I'm not planning to run away, and I can't even think of a reason why I would. But I also couldn't ignore what was going on."

Jason seemed hurt that she hadn't told him her reasons. Maya hadn't intended to hurt him, but Pallavi, her brother, and dad deserved the opportunity tell their own story. If only she could get them to come here. And that was really the big problem. Maya was stuck in the middle between the people here, who might help strangers, and the strangers who would rather steal than ask for help.

CHAPTER TWENTY-ONE

The sun was rising, and Jason was still bugging her to tell him the truth. By now, Pallavi would be looking for the medicine. Maya couldn't just leave them wondering, and she couldn't get away. She only had one choice.

"Jason, you have to promise you will keep the secret," she said.

"Is it going to get me in trouble?"

"Only if they know that I told you and you didn't pass on the information. I promise, I'll be the one in trouble." How much worse could it get? She was under guard twenty-four hours a day.

"Is it something that might hurt us?" Jason asked, leaning in close again so they could whisper.

Maya didn't think any harm would come to them. If someone needed the pills, there were still enough. And one of the alliances would provide replacements. "No, but if we don't do something, it will hurt some other people."

Jason nodded his head. "Okay, I won't tell anyone."

Maya hoped this time he'd be able to do it.

She shared what she knew about Pallavi and what they needed. "I think we should try to get them to join us here. It would be great to have another kid our age, and Pallavi is almost the same age as Mellow. But she's not ready yet, and I think her dad is too sick to move."

"I'm not stealing pills for her," Jason said.

"No, but you could go to the place I was supposed to leave them and leave a note." Maya scrambled out of bed and dug into her desk drawer. "I'll write it and seal it in an envelope, so you won't know what I say if anyone asks." Jason frowned. "Not that anyone will. Nobody suspects you. You could go for a walk, say you are foraging, and there will be no questions."

"I should say no, but you'll just find a way to go yourself, right?"

Maya smiled. She had won. "Probably. I don't think they can keep up this punishment for long. It would just be better if Pallavi knew that I was still trying."

"Write the note. I'll go right after I get off guard shift. How far away is it? Do I need to take something to eat? Will I be able to do some foraging while I'm gone? I need to bring something back or they will get suspicious." He watched her write the note. "You can let me see what it is."

Maya was hunched over the paper, so her brother couldn't read the contents. "I think it would be better if you didn't." She folded the paper and slid it into an envelope. "The less you know about this the better for you."

She handed him the message. "It's not that far, and you can forage. It's important that you leave the message in the little cave and then go. Don't hang around, and don't try to meet Pallavi."

"Why?" Jason tucked the envelope into his pocket. "Maybe I can convince her to come here."

"No. She's real cautious. I don't want you scaring her away." She waited until Jason nodded before she slipped back into her bed. "When is someone coming to relieve you?"

"Any time now. It will be Mom," he said. "She was pretty mad last night, maybe you should pretend to be asleep while she's here."

Maya curled up on her side and pulled the blanket around herself. "Yeah. But she always knows when I'm pretending. And if she's mad she won't care if I'm asleep, she'll just wake me up and give me a lecture."

The door opened, and her mom walked through without even knocking. Maya watched her brother leave through tears. Her mom didn't think she'd earned a little privacy. It was like she was only a kid again. She was almost ten for gosh sakes.

Pallavi waited behind a large tree, watching the boy and hoping he would go soon. But he didn't. She knew Maya wasn't to be trusted. This boy knew where to leave whatever he'd brought. It wasn't medicine, just an envelope.

The boy, it must be Maya's brother, put the envelope inside and then started poking around, looking at the ground around the cave. Not the rocks, but the earth and muddy grass.

He brushed a few leaves aside and then looked up at the brush in front of where he was crouched. Shaking his head, he returned to the search on the ground.

Pallavi heard a noise behind her. She didn't know where to look. At the boy, or whoever was approaching? *Is it a trap?*

The boy hadn't noticed anything, he was busy clearing space in the dirt. Pallavi risked a glance behind.

Mahir!

She was surrounded by stupid brothers.

Holding her finger to her lips, she pointed to a thicket of low bushes and waited until Mahir was safely hidden before turning back to the stranger.

"Why are you letting Maya be punished for you?" He was staring directly at her. "You can both come out. I won't tell anyone you're here. I won't hurt you."

Mahir stepped out from cover before Pallavi could tell him to run. "Your sister was helping. We didn't ask her to do it, so it's not our fault she's in trouble."

Pallavi wasn't in the mood to let them butt heads. She moved into the clearing, waving Mahir to join her. "What's your name?"

"Jason. Didn't Maya tell you about me?" He sounded a bit hurt.

"She said she had a brother. But you don't look much like her. I just wanted to be sure."

"Yeah, I look like my dad. She looks like Mom," he said. "So, why is Maya taking the punishment?"

Pallavi smiled, recognizing the stubborn look and stance. She'd seen it plenty of times on Mahir's face. Jason looked about the same age, maybe a couple of years older. She could see the signs in him of lanky teenager; the softness of childhood hardening. She'd never seen another biracial kid, and if she didn't know Maya, she wouldn't have known he was anything but African American, if that meant anything now. "I didn't know she was in trouble."

Jason looked at Mahir rather than answer her unspoken question. "Who are you? I know this is Pallavi, are you her brother?"

Mahir nodded. Apparently, he wasn't ready to make friends. Jason would make a good one for Mahir, Pallavi thought. "Yes, he's Mahir, my brother. What happened to Maya?"

"They caught her sneaking out pills for you. She's grounded, and someone is watching her all the time because they think she's going to run away, or something."

Pallavi's heart sank. There would be no medicine for her dad. He wasn't getting better, and she knew she was denying the truth. She wanted to keep Mahir from realizing what was going to happen. The pills probably wouldn't help, but she couldn't stop trying to find something to make him better.

"You should go back," she said. "They'll let Maya out eventually. You can tell her that she doesn't need to worry, we'll find what we need."

She stood and grabbed Mahir's arm, ready to run back to the shelter as soon as Jason was out of sight. She couldn't let him know where the shelter was because there was still time to save Dad.

"I'm not going anywhere, Pallavi," her brother said.

Didn't he understand that they had to go?

"We need to get back to Dad," Pallavi said. "When Jason goes, we'll head back."

"I'm not stupid," Mahir said, pulling his arm out of her grasp. "I know what you want to do. It's wrong. You should help Maya. She helped us and now she's in trouble."

Her brother's stubborn streak was going to get him in real trouble one day. "Maya is fine. She's home and they won't punish her forever."

Mahir moved to stand beside Jason. "If you aren't going to get her out of trouble, then I am. She's keeping our secret."

She couldn't let Mahir go to the farm. He'd spoil everything. They wouldn't let him come back and she'd be alone with Dad. She wouldn't be able to go find more medicine, she wouldn't be able to forage for fresh supplies. "We can't leave the shelter."

Jason was watching them, and Pallavi wished he was gone. If they were alone it would be easy to sway Mahir.

"You're afraid we won't let you go," Jason said. "If you come and tell us why you made Maya steal, you think we'll lock you up. And your dad would suffer."

"Are you saying your friends would happily let us go back?" Pallavi asked the question to stall for time, she wouldn't be naïve enough to believe Jason.

He shrugged. "I don't know what will happen. We haven't had to do anything like this before."

At least he was honest. "Maya thought we needed help. She thought it was important that no one know."

"Yes, Pallavi, and now she needs us." Mahir's fists were clenched again. She hated him being in that state.

"What do you want me to do?" Pallavi asked. This had to stop. If she was going to find medication for Dad, she would need to go much farther than before. It was going to mean being away for at least a couple of days. And Mahir needed to be with Dad. "I can't go rescue her."

Mahir sighed and turned to Jason. "I'm sorry she's so stubborn. I wish she wasn't right."

"Yeah, I guess there's no easy way out of this," Jason said.

Mahir looked like he wanted to hug Jason, but he held back. "If Pallavi promises to stop asking Maya to help, would that be good enough?"

It would be hard, but they could find food growing around the shelter, and maybe she could still take it from the farm.

"And, if you could say it was okay to tell your secret, it would get her out of trouble. That's mostly why she's being punished, because she won't tell them why."

"And will you tell them?" Pallavi asked. Now that Jason knew, their location might not stay hidden for long.

"No, I promised Maya I wouldn't. Plus, I don't really know the story. And we don't know where you live, so telling isn't going to put you in any more danger."

"Pallavi, don't be so mean. Let Maya tell them," Mahir said. He was staring at her as if to plant his words in her brain.

If she could say no, it would be the best case for them. They could stay hidden until they absolutely had to leave the shelter. As soon as the adults at the farm knew there was another family in the area, they would start looking. It didn't matter if they came to help, or to punish. As soon as they saw Dad, they'd be afraid of catching his disease. "I won't ask Maya for help anymore," she said.

"And," Mahir prompted.

Everything was a risk. The shelter was well hidden, and Dad wouldn't be sick much longer. And beneath all the logic, Pallavi couldn't let Maya be punished for helping. "How do you plan to convince her that I said she didn't have to keep the secret?"

Jason took a sheet of paper and a pencil out of his pocket and held it out for Pallavi to take. "Write her a note, and put something in there that only you would know. I'll take it back."

Pallavi found a flat rock to support the paper. When she was done, she handed the note back to Jason. "Please, don't come looking for us."

She waited with Mahir until Jason was out of sight and then they ran for the shelter.

CHAPTER TWENTY-TWO

Jason had been in Maya's room for too long for Ava's comfort. They were up to something. She should have taken Jason off the rotation of guards, but she'd been sorry for Maya and thought that having her brother might help her come to the right decision.

When Jason went in, Ava had sent Tik away and listened at the door, feeling a flush of shame at spying on her kids. Kids who were getting old enough to have secrets from her.

The door hadn't let much through, but Ava heard Jason say that someone was okay, and she'd given him a note. Maya had responded with something about 'only if I have to'.

Then she heard a board creak. Ava pulled away from her listening post to lean on the wall opposite just as Jason opened the door.

"Mom, you can't keep her there forever," he said. No greeting, nothing.

Ava wanted to let her daughter out, but Maya needed to give them something. "Is she going to talk?"

"Don't make her," he said. "Mom, you know Maya wouldn't do

something like this without a good reason. She can't tell you, but I promise she won't do it again."

It felt wrong to talk about Maya outside her bedroom — who was she kidding, outside her prison. "Let's go downstairs. Maya will be fine for a little bit."

In the kitchen, Ava made a pot of tea and poured a glass of milk for Jason. When they were settled, and she'd had time to think through her feelings, she started talking, "It's not just us, Jason. The rest of the community needs to believe Maya can be trusted. Do you know the reason she won't tell us?"

She saw the flash across her son's face. He'd considered lying. When had she lost control of her kid's moral core?

"Yes, I do. I won't start stealing, don't freak. But I can't tell you, Mom. It's not my secret. It's not Maya's secret. We both promised not to tell. Would you want us to go back on our word?"

Stealing medication was a big problem; was it big enough to make one of them talk? In reality, the medication was getting stale, and they had books to tell them how to make natural substitutes for most of them. If they kept all the pills, they would be worthless in about six months according to Deb. Making Maya break her promise would make a wound in their relationship that would never go away.

Ava sighed. It was so easy, even last year, to raise these kids. Being on the farm seemed to mature them fast. She didn't regret bringing them here. By now, in New Surrey, they would be recruited into gangs, or being groomed to work for the government. And in retrospect, the government was just another gang.

"I'll talk to the others. You will be responsible for your sister's behavior. I can't just let her go, you know that." Ava reached out to take Jason's hand, but he drew it away and sat on it. "Fine, I get that you don't like me much right now. Are you willing to keep your sister on the straight and narrow?"

Jason looked down at the table, Ava hoped he was considering his answer. Maya wouldn't take well to the restriction.

"I promise that I won't let Maya do anything stupid," Jason said.

Ava knew he was trying to find a loophole. "Okay, we'll talk at dinner and, if everyone agrees, she can come out this evening."

Evan stood beside Scott on the hill approaching Redstone. The journey had been boring, thankfully so. They'd seen a few of Cole's men ranging the hills, but two well-armed men were not on their list of prey. Evan knew that would change as the Fort grew stronger; he hoped the alliances would be in place before that.

"Looks like we can't just wander in," Scott said pointing to the four guards facing them with weapons drawn.

"That's good. They know how to deal with threats." Evan put his own weapons on display. "Who does the talking?" He'd been given the task of opening negotiations, but Scott represented the farm.

"It's your show." Scott took his own guns and made a display of unloading them.

The guards beckoned them forward. It was awkward leading the horse and carrying his guns. They reached the guards who waited about fifty feet from the gates to the town. The wall was new, made of scrap metal, old beams and barbed wire, it would hold back most attacks. Setting a fire would be the way to destroy the fortification, but the wood was soaked and wouldn't catch easily.

"Your business?" The lead guard asked.

Redstone was built across the main access road. Anyone traveling through would be at the mercy of these men, or face a long and difficult detour.

"We are here to speak with whoever leads the town," Evan said.

"About what?" The guard didn't change his expression. He wasn't interested, just going through a script of questions.

"That's between us and your...?"

"Mayor and council," the guard said.

"I don't think they would appreciate us giving the details to you." Evan wanted to test the limits of the man's patience. The other three, a man and two women, lifted their guns; not aiming them at Scott and Evan exactly, but no longer harmlessly pointing at the ground.

"I think they appreciate us doing our job and not letting any riffraff into the town."

"How do you tell the riffraff from someone with legitimate business?" Evan looked around. "There doesn't seem to be much traffic through here."

The guard sighed. "Most riffraff are smart asses. And you seem to be a smart ass. What's your name, and does your buddy here talk at all?"

"Evan White. Scott here does talk, but we didn't want to confuse you with a lot of chatter."

"See, smart ass talk. I'm bored with this. Tell me where you came from and why you need to see the mayor. We'll send word and if they agree to let you in, then I'll stand aside."

"Scott's from a farming community a bit west from here. I'm from a place called Prosperity; north to the river and then east a few days. We want to talk about dealing with Newton Cole up at the Fort."

The guard narrowed his eyes at Evan. He turned and gave orders to one of the women and she ran through the city gate. "Back up to the crest of that hill." The guard pointed to where Evan had first seen Redstone. "I wouldn't count on it. We have a bunch of citizens who came through Prosperity, when you called yourselves The Community of Hope."

Evan didn't answer the implied accusation. He'd make the usual apologies for his community to the leaders, not a guard.

At the crest of the hill, Scott hobbled the horses so they could eat, and dug out some travel rations. "Might as well get comfortable. I think the guard is wrong. They will be curious about what we have to offer. Just need to make us wait to punish us for your town's actions."

CHAPTER TWENTY-THREE

The guard wasn't happy when he rode up after only a few minutes to take them to the council. Evan didn't respond to the man's irritation as they passed through the gates. If he wanted people to believe his town had changed, he couldn't take offense easily — probably at all.

The council turned out to be three women. Each representing a function of running a town. They'd introduced themselves. Mary Franklin was the mayor, Ellen Moonchild oversaw the financial well-being of Redstone, and Lela O'Brien looked after the productivity.

"Why did they send you to us?" mayor Franklin asked. She kept her attention on Evan, ignoring Scott.

"The people on the farm are looking to make alliances. I'm here to find out if you're willing to start negotiations." He knew she meant why him, and not someone who actually lived on the farm. He hadn't come up with a way to explain that. He couldn't say he was being tested. How would that feel to these women? To be part of a test of a potential ally.

"Why would we?" Ellen Moonchild asked. "We are strong and protected by our wall. We have farms that produce what we need.

We have plans for a future. What does the farm, with its small population bring to us?"

He felt Scott bristle at the implication that the farm was not worthy of their notice. Evan didn't look at Scott. If this was going to be successful, they had to think he was empowered to speak. "There are several reasons why you need alliances. Your walls will not stand up to a concerted attack. Your long-term plans will come to nothing if you are overrun."

"You mean the Fort," Mayor Franklin asked.

"Right now, the Fort. But there will always be someone who thinks they can take what you have because they are stronger or better armed, or have less to lose."

"How will a handful of people a two-day ride away help us against an attack?" Lela O'Brien asked. "No one is close enough to come to anyone's aid."

"That's our strength," Evan said. "It would take a huge army to take us all out at the same time. Yes, it will be difficult to come to the aid of an ally, but if we band together we can gather intelligence that might give us that time." It wasn't working. He could tell that the women were thinking only about the threat in front of them. "The real benefit is long term," he added. "Look at where everyone is in this area. Smallholdings and farms, and communities like Redstone. If we don't band together, we will fall to the Fort one at a time. How will you defend against the Fort when all of your neighbors are taken first?"

The mayor looked to the other women in turn. There was an unspoken question. Something they had agreed before entering the room. She received small nods from each of her co-leaders. "What you say makes sense. I see why we would need to make alliances, but why the farm?"

This couldn't be what they had agreed. It was too simple a question. "The farm sits at the center between us. Prosperity, Crystal, and Redstone are the outer boundaries of the circle. Inside are more individuals than you might think. If the farm linked up with the smallholders around them, they would be larger than Prosperity, or Crystal." He left them to consider how small Redstone might feel in that circumstance. "The smallholders are within range of any of us if help is needed. The farm is the only community that can bring them into an alliance. They tend to look on offers from towns with suspicion."

This time the mayor nodded. She'd bought the logic, but there was still something in the way of agreement.

"Why are you not here on behalf of Prosperity?" The mayor asked.

"I am authorized to work with the farm," he said. "We know our reputation. If we thought you would agree, an agent would be knocking on your gate."

"So, you think an alliance with the farm will whitewash Prosperity's history?" This from Councilor Moonchild.

Evan felt his face flush with shame. He ignored the urge to apologize. "It's not to whitewash, it's to atone."

The mayor looked to the others again, then stood. "If the farm wishes to negotiate an alliance, they can send Lena or Ava: they are the leaders. We do not negotiate with agents."

Moonchild and O'Brien stood with the mayor and all three marched from the room. The guard who had been standing in the corner gestured for Evan and Scott to follow.

Evan knew it wasn't the best outcome, but if Lena could go to Redstone, then they might agree to an alliance. Two hours on the road back — when he should be headed for Prosperity — and Scott had barely spoken. Evan couldn't stand it any longer with the anxiety about his future relationships with the farm on the line. They were riding together, keeping an eye out for any sign of Cole's men, so he kept his voice low. "Will Lena go?"

Scott glanced at him and then returned his focus to the edges of the trees. "Why do you think it will be Lena?"

Evan, encouraged by the question when he'd expected a grunt, or simple yes or no, answered, "Ava won't leave her kids. Or am I reading that wrong?"

Scott chuckled. "No, you got that right. Something's up with Maya, there's no way Ava would leave. Even if she did, I don't think she'd have the patience to negotiate."

"So?"

"Yeah, Lena will go. I'll come with her, or Keith. The roads won't stay this quiet much longer."

Evan nodded his agreement. Cole would be escalating soon. "I could come, too. I need to get an answer and get back to Prosperity, but I could stay for this."

Scott looked at Evan's damaged hand. "You won't be much help. Just the two of us, yeah; you can still fire a weapon, but anything larger, your injury would be more of a hindrance."

The hand throbbed in response to the words. Evan wanted to deny it, and it was healing, but Scott was right. He could probably fire a couple of times, then his hand would stop working.

"I was thinking," Scott said. "The farm could use some more meat. I could hunt on the way back."

"Won't that slow us down?"

"Not us. You need to take the message back to the farm. Since Cole's men don't seem to be on the prowl, we can risk separating. If you ride hard, it's only a day, maybe less." Scott lifted the bag of trail food from his pommel. "You take this, I'll forage. Give me the arrows."

Evan couldn't pull a bow, but he'd been carrying an extra quiver for Scott. He wanted to argue. His gut said it was too dangerous to split up. That maybe Cole's men were waiting for just this. There was no way to do it without sounding like a coward. He'd made it from Prosperity to the farm without a problem. A day's hard ride couldn't be riskier than that. It might reinforce that Prosperity was worth an alliance; he had to risk it. "Okay. How far behind me do you think you'll be?" He took the sack of food and hung it on his own pommel, then untied the quiver. It was only then that he realized he'd automatically used the same hand, even though it was awkward.

"A day, maybe less if I get a deer." As soon as he secured the quiver, Scott nodded goodbye and urged his horse off the road.

Within moments, Evan was alone, sitting on his horse in the middle of the road. Like a target. He lowered his body and squeezed his knees; his horse went from stationary, to canter, to gallop.

This is when I miss my car. A car can go at speed until it runs out of gas. The horse couldn't gallop all day without hurting it. Evan was in a hurry, but not so much that he'd destroy the animal.

He found a grassy space with a pond and dismounted. He bit into the trail bar, and the horse stuck his head into the pond. He promised himself it would only be a few minutes. They'd go slower and keep riding longer for the next stretch. If he was careful, he'd make the farm by late morning, deliver his report and sleep.

His hand throbbed. As he chewed the last bite of his dry bar, he peeled off the bandage. There was some swelling, but the wound looked like it was healing. There was no discoloration, no angry red lines of infection. When he got back on the road, he'd try to hold the hand up so that the swelling would go down, and maybe it would hurt less.

A twig snapped. His horse backed away, snorting.

Evan ran for the rifle he'd left attached to the saddle.

Too late.

Three men stepped into the clearing. Not Cole's men. The guards from Redstone. Unless Redstone was already in league with the Fort...

"Don't try it," the guard they'd spoken to this morning said.

"I'm just as happy to pull the trigger and save us the effort of bringing you back."

Evan took one step, hoping the threat was empty.

A shot, the bullet digging a hole in the grass six inches from his foot. His horse reared and then took off at a gallop. Food, water, weapons, and the ointment for his hand, all gone. Would the animal head for the farm? Prosperity? Or just run wild?

"Why?" Evan asked. "What did I do?"

The guard didn't answer, just nodded to his companions. They took Evan and tied his hands, causing him to grunt in pain as they grabbed his injured palm. They pushed him toward the trees, giving him a jab with the butt of a rifle when he stumbled.

"Look, this must be a mistake," he said as they marched him along an animal path between the trunks. "I've done nothing. I'm just following your mayor's orders."

The first guard laughed. "Me too. Shut up and it will go easier."

They had reached a wagon, horses tied to a branch of the last tree in the line. "Get in," the guard said.

In the bed of the wagon, they tied Evan's legs and threw a blanket over him. He breathed in sawdust, horse sweat and manure.

"The mayor is going to punish you for what your town did," the guard said, his words muffled by the heavy blanket. "You can change the name, but it doesn't wipe out the history."

Evan closed his eyes and tried to breathe through his nose. There was no point talking until he got in front of the mayor.

He hoped Scott would get to the farm soon. And that they might think of rescuing him when it looked like he was in trouble. But maybe they'd figure he'd run off and no one would be coming.

CHAPTER TWENTY-FOUR

The wagon traveled much slower than a horse. Evan heard the muffled sounds of a heated conversation between his captors, but no actual words. The temperature dropped at what must have been nightfall. The stink from the blanket kept his hunger at bay, but that was all. By the time the wagon rocked to a stop, there was no joint or muscle that didn't scream with pain. His hand no longer throbbed; it was a ball of constant pain at the end of his arm.

The blanket came off and his restraints were undone. Evan's eyes slammed shut against the bright glare of the lights. Redstone had found a way to make and use electricity.

"He's half dead," the mayor said.

Evan forced his eyes open. They were in what must have been a classroom before. A blackboard still occupied the wall at the front, a couple of desk chairs were scattered around. His captors stood together by the door.

"He'll draw sympathy in this state," she said. There was no sympathy in her voice. She poked his shoulder, and smiled when he moaned. "Get him fixed up. We're better than the Community of Hope, Evan. See how we make sure you can defend yourself. We don't skip the trial and steal everything."

There was no point in arguing here. If there was a trial, Evan would make his arguments and hope it wasn't just a formality. The mayor didn't give him any time, just turned on her heel and left them.

"Told ya, Irv," the younger of the men said. "Shoulda just killed him, save the trouble."

Irv, the lead guard, turned on him. "We are the good guys, Pete. You want to behave like that, go join Newton at the Fort." He glared until Pete looked away. "Come on, the doc will be waiting."

Two hours later, Evan was alone in a small room that held a bed and a chair. The pain numbed by a salve and his hand properly bandaged, Evan lay back ready for sleep. If his trial was going to be in the morning, he needed the rest.

As soon as he closed his eyes, a klaxon sounded. He heard feet running and his door swung open, slamming into the wall and bouncing back to hit the mayor on the shoulder.

"What's happening?" Evan asked, not wanting to be shut down before he could get in a word.

"As if you didn't know," the mayor said. "The Fort. Cole's sent a handful of his men against us. They are armed to the teeth and we aren't prepared."

"You think I would bring them here?" Evan scrambled to his feet. "Why would I come to make an alliance if I was part of Cole's force?"

"You came to find our weaknesses," she said. "Tie him up."

Irv didn't move. "Are you sure? If they get in, he won't be able to get away."

"And if I'm right and we leave him free, he can attack from behind."

Her eyes were blazing. Evan had seen that before in Abigail. If he could break her rage, he might be able to turn her off the path. "I swear I'm not with them." He held up his hand. "I got this spying on them."

"Prove it." She wasn't cooling down.

"I can't, and you know that." He looked to Irv. "How long did you follow us?"

"A while. We knew Scott. We've been doing some scouting. We didn't know you except from the survivors we took in."

Evan wished he'd been more talkative with Scott, said something Irv could have overheard. "So, Scott seemed comfortable with me, right?"

"Yep."

Evan turned to the mayor. "Do you think Scott would have been with me if I was one of Cole's men?"

The question stalled her rage. It wasn't exactly calm, but he'd derailed her determination to blame him.

"Let me fight for you," Evan said. "Another gun, even one with a damaged hand, will help. If you don't send them off now, they'll keep coming back hoping to wear you down."

"That will happen anyway," she said.

"Yeah, but if you beat them right now, they'll wait until they are stronger. In that time, you can make alliances and we can fight them together."

The mayor looked from Evan to Irv, chewing her lip. The passion drained as she tried to make up her mind. It was a tactic that worked on Abigail in the beginning.

"You fight alongside Irv. Don't leave his side." She didn't wait for a response.

"Get your ass out here," Irv said.

It looked like Cole's men were testing Redstone. Sure, if they got lucky, they'd take it, but there weren't enough of them to take over easily. And in Evan's experience, men like Newton Cole always wanted it easy.

The fighting was contained just inside the gates. Keeping it that way should be a simple matter of numbers. It turned out that Cole did a better job of training his fighters. They didn't miss often. Redstone was a different matter. Evan recognized the problem quickly because Prosperity had fallen prey to it in the early days — back when they were the Community of Hope. It was all theory. When the enemy fought back, it was hard to keep your training in mind. They would be better the next time.

"If we can get behind that building," he said to Irv, pointing to a solid brick house halfway to the gate, "we can cut them off, and maybe take them prisoner."

Irv checked the path. "You planning to run and let me give cover?" His words dripped with suspicion.

Evan wondered what it would take to get Irv past what happened before Abigail was gone. Saving the man's life four times in this skirmish obviously wasn't enough.

"You think we can make it together?" When Irv rolled his eyes, Evan continued. "You can go while I provide cover. It's more dangerous, but I'm happy to go second."

Irv glanced at the path again. Evan could see him calculating the odds. "Fine, you go first. If you try to escape, or join those bastards, I'll empty my weapon into you. Got it?"

Evan had no intention of doing either. The only way to make Redstone see the sense of an alliance, even with Prosperity, was to prove he was trustworthy, and capable.

The attackers were reloading in turns, so there was no break in their shots. Evan tucked his damaged hand under his body and made sure his rifle was safe. The bullets flew mostly at head height for someone kneeling, so he lay on the ground and rolled until he was behind the shell of a pickup truck. Checking again, he crawled the few feet to another obstruction and paused to look back. Irv was firing toward the enemy, and looking directly at Evan.

The building — probably a house before, by the layout — was empty and only a few feet away. Evan had to cross that space without any cover. The low wall in front meant he couldn't roll or crawl. This was going to be a suicide run.

A glance at Irv gained him a nod. He shot wildly, and Evan ran. He made it to the side of the building. Looking back, Irv was already running to join him.

Evan aimed his rifle at the man crouched behind an abandoned wagon. The attackers had tipped it to provide them with a little protection. From his vantage, Evan could just see the side of one of Cole's men.

He aimed and squeezed the trigger.

The man fell. He couldn't be dead. There was no way Evan would have hit anything vital.

"Shit, that's the hardest ten yards I've ever run," Irv said, panting as he raised his own weapon.

They fired a few more times, but it was clear that the men from the Fort weren't going to continue. One by one they dodged bullets until they were through the gate and headed for the Fort.

Evan ran to stop them from escaping, but they were already mounted and headed for the road. He didn't want to chance hitting a horse. They were too valuable.

He lowered his rifle as Irv joined him.

"I think the doc overmedicated you," Irv said.

Evan frowned. What the hell was he talking about? Then pain lanced through his arm. He reached to grab the muscle and felt the wet, sticky blood running. He blinked and felt his knees buckle. Then everything went black.

CHAPTER TWENTY-FIVE

It was four days since Pallavi gave her dad the first pills. She could no longer hide the fact that they weren't working. By now, this fever should have broken, but he was still bathed in sweat. She couldn't get enough water down him to prevent dehydration, and trying to get him to eat was just wasting food.

"Is there stronger medicine somewhere?" Mahir asked. He replaced the cold, wet cloth that had turned warm on their father's forehead. He looked up at Pallavi and she could see the fear in his eyes. Mahir's skin was showing the effects of lack of sleep; pale except for the dark circles around his eyes. Everything that was happening was aging him too quickly. Helplessness over-whelmed her, so she busied herself cleaning up.

"Pallavi, maybe their medicine has gone bad."

"It might be the wrong kind of medicine," Pallavi said quietly. She was glad Mahir was there. He might be a pest sometimes, but she wouldn't want to do this alone. "I... Maybe I can find a clinic, or pharmacy. Maybe there was a hospital in the area."

"Did you see one when Dad brought us here?" Mahir helped her carry everything into the kitchen to be washed. "I wish I had been old enough to remember and see what was nearby."

Pallavi had been old enough, but the times were crazy. Dad had hidden them in the back of the van, so she hadn't been able to see what was around. He'd driven them for almost a whole day before pulling over and hustling them into the shelter. "I don't know. There must be something. We know there were farms around here, and there were some towns. There must be at least a clinic." The only other place that might have supplies was the Fort, but she couldn't go there. She'd never come back, no matter what medicine they had.

"I guess I have to stay here and look after Dad," Mahir said.

"I'll try not to be away too long," Pallavi said, grateful that there was no argument coming from Mahir. "I know it's going to be hard, but you can do it. There's still some medicine that you can give him. I know it's not helping, or not helping much, but it can't hurt. Just keep him cleaned up and try to get him to drink lots of water. Maybe give him some plain rice. He needs his strength." She had to stop talking, because tears closed her throat. She needed to be strong in front of her brother.

They cleaned up in silence. But Pallavi could almost hear Mahir's thoughts rolling around in his mind. He kept throwing glances at her and then seemed almost ready to speak. It was a relief when he didn't. If he gave her too much resistance, she might become cowardly enough to stay and watch her father die.

"You don't think that the medicine will be gone?" Mahir finally asked.

Pallavi focused on putting away the dishes they just cleaned so she wouldn't have to look at her brother as she spoke. "I'll go east. I think there's a town out there, everyone we know of is west of us. Maybe there'll be some places that haven't been cleaned out. Even if all the medicine is gone, maybe I can find a book telling us how to treat him without medication.

In the background, her father started coughing again. Every wheeze that triggered another cough tore at her heart.

"There's another way," Mahir said, touching Pallavi's arm to make her turn. "We can go to the farm. They have a nurse there."

And Dad wouldn't be our responsibility any longer. Pallavi didn't know if Mahir realized that's what it sounded like. "And they might decide to move us along. Who would take in a man that sick? They might think he has a new plague. They won't care that we look healthy. If they kick us out where would we go?"

"If you don't come back, what will happen to us?" Mahir walked away before she could answer.

Mahir watched Pallavi disappear into the line of trees. It was a full moon tonight, so she should be okay. He went from the opening in the back of the shelter to check on his dad. For the first time in days, he seemed to be sleeping peacefully. He still had a fever, but he wasn't as restless. He would be okay for a little while. Mahir couldn't just sit safe in the shelter while she was out there. He was her brother; it was his job to take care of her.

He promised himself he wouldn't go too far. If he knew that Pallavi had made it through the trees, maybe he'd be able to sleep while she was gone. He wasn't sure what road she was going to take to get to this pharmacy that she thought might be there, but he'd find out when she got there. That's what he would do, track her until she was safely on the road. Then he'd come back. That way he'd know where to go look for her when he got worried about how long she'd been gone. He gave his dad a kiss on the forehead and whispered, "I love you."

Mahir slipped through the opening in the back of the shelter. The moonlight that helped him feel better as he watched Pallavi now made him feel exposed. He ran for the safety of the trees, stopping only when he was in the shadows.

One thing that he was really good at, thanks to his following Pallavi on her adventures, was tracking. His sister was good at hiding her tracks, but he was better than she was. A newly broken branch on a bush told him which route she had taken. Maybe he should catch up to her and let her know to be more careful.

The trees weren't very thick, so there were lots of places where the light got through. He just didn't feel exposed here because there was always a place to hide.

After about five minutes, he saw Pallavi moving ahead of him. He didn't hear any noise as she went, which made him feel a little less worried. He held back, not wanting to get caught. She needed to be focused on what she was doing, not worried that he was running around. He may only be a kid, but he knew it was dangerous out here if you were not careful.

She never noticed him. Mahir figured it had been about half an hour. It had gotten a lot colder since he started out. But Pallavi still didn't even know he was there. He knew that meant he was tracking her properly, but part of him wanted her to know. Not that he wanted her to worry, but maybe she could go knowing she wasn't alone. The trees thinned, and the ground changed from being all broken up by the roots, to smoother, and then he was through the tree line and standing on grass.

Mahir took a step back so that he wasn't as exposed. The road was there across the dry ditch. Pallavi was crouched in the ditch, her head cocked to the side, listening.

He would stay here until she disappeared down the road.

There wasn't much cover for her, but that couldn't be helped. If she stayed in the ditch and ran bent over, maybe that would be enough cover. At night, Mahir didn't think there was too much traffic, but if people were out they were probably not the kind that she should meet.

He watched her climb out of the ditch onto the road. He almost cried out for her to stay down. He had to believe she knew what she was doing; the road would be faster.

The road ran straight for a long way. Mahir would not be able to see Pallavi to the end, but he couldn't just return to the shelter. About a hundred yards down, the road passed between two hillocks, like they'd had to blast through to get the road to run flat. Mahir made a deal with himself; when she was on the other side, he would turn back to the shelter.

Pallavi ran straight through the gap. Mahir made himself take the first step home.

Then he heard a scream.

In the distance, he saw two men on horses chasing Pallavi. One of them scooped her up across the saddle. The horses sped up, and before Mahir could react, Pallavi was gone.

CHAPTER TWENTY-SIX

There was no way he could chase after the men. And even if he could, he was just a kid, and they probably had guns. All Mahir could do was run back to the shelter. Maybe Dad would be awake, not to rescue her, but at least to tell Mahir what to do.

He didn't care about how much noise he made now. He crashed through the undergrowth and bounced off some trees as he took the shortest route back. He should have never let Pallavi go. He knew it was dangerous. He told her it was dangerous. He hated everything about the way they lived.

As he approached the shelter, Mahir slowed down and tried to catch his breath. He couldn't waste time trying to gasp out his story. His legs were shaky, but he kept going. No matter how much his body protested, it was nothing like what Pallavi was going through. He didn't really know what might be happening, but he knew it would be bad.

He reached the corner of the shelter, for the first time noticing how little they were hidden. Only a few bushes and trees blocked anyone from seeing the building, and since they'd been going in and out, he could see a path starting to wear in the grass.

When Pallavi was safe, they would have to find a way to make the shelter invisible again.

He slid through the gap, noticing the boards were getting smooth from the friction. Even Dad was going to notice soon that there was an exit here. He would be mad, but mad is better than sick.

"Dad? Are you awake?" There was no answer, but his dad wasn't wheezing anymore. That had to be a good sign.

Mahir crept across the small space, not wanting to startle his dad if he was asleep. He was still bundled under the blankets like he hadn't moved since they left. He reached out his hand to shake him. "Dad. Dad, wake up."

It didn't feel right. Now that his own breathing was under control, he realized he couldn't hear his dad's. Something cold lodged in Mahir's belly. He reached out again, this time pulling the blanket away. His dad didn't move.

He didn't want to believe it, but Mahir knew the truth. His dad's skin looked kind of yellowed, and flat. There was no shine to his cheeks.

Dad was dead.

He didn't have time to cry. He didn't even try CPR; his dad was cold. But Pallavi was alive, he wouldn't let himself believe she wasn't. And Mahir had to figure out how to rescue her.

Sleepless nights were getting more common. Ava took a sip of her whiskey and closed her eyes. In some part of her, she'd imagined life on a farm as less stressful that in the city. Hard work, yes, and that's what helped her to fall asleep most nights, but lately all she seemed to do was wait. Wait for news about the alliances, wait for Evan and Scott to return, wait for Maya to tell her the truth, and wait to find out who was taking their supplies.

If she was honest, Maya was the reason she was up this late.

The little sounds of the night filled her mind with calm. If it weren't for the bugs and the roaming thugs from the Fort, she'd just sleep on the porch. Maybe sometime in the future. Tonight, almost tomorrow morning, she sat with a glass of booze and a rifle.

The peace of the night was working its magic, and Ava was ready to pack up and go to bed when footsteps crunched on the gravel walkway.

She grabbed the rifle, aware of the danger of handling a gun after a glass or two of whiskey and stood. "Step into the light."

The intruder obeyed. A young boy, maybe a little younger than Jason, stepped forward. He was thin, and undersized. His brown skin pale, his large brown eyes sunken, signs of recent tears on his cheeks.

"Who are you?" Her voice was a little gentler this time. This boy wasn't a threat; unless he was bait in a trap, but she didn't sense anyone lurking.

"Mahir Kingman. I lived with my dad and sister in a shelter over there." He pointed to the east.

"Lived? What happened?"

He hitched a sigh and rubbed his cheeks. "My dad died, and my sister... she was trying to find more medicine and two men kidnapped her."

The mystery of the missing supplies was solved. Ava put the rifle on the floor of the porch. "You'd better come in."

He stood his ground. "No, I came for help. Someone has to save Pallavi. Those men will hurt her. She's all I have." Tears streamed despite his obvious efforts to stop them.

"Come inside and I'll wake up the others. We'll figure it out."

His shoulders slumped. "Okay."

She locked the door behind her and took Mahir to the kitchen. "Are you hungry?" He nodded, so she pulled a jug of milk out of the icebox and poured a glass. She made him a peanut butter sandwich after checking on his allergies. "You eat that while I get everyone up."

He nodded and stuffed the sandwich in his mouth.

Ava woke Keith first, sending him and Deb down to check on Mahir while she explained the situation to the rest of the group.

In the kitchen, Ava saw Keith sitting next to Mahir, talking quietly. The boy seemed more confident now. Deb was filling a bowl with soapy water. She looked up as the room began to fill. "He's healthy, just a few scratches that need cleaning before they get infected."

Keith patted Mahir on the arm and stood. "It sounds like Newton Cole's men. They are getting bolder. And they're moving east. I can start now and track her, maybe get her back." He looked at Mahir. "I think they won't hurt her, they'll take her back to Cole."

Ava hoped so, but even if they did what everyone expected, she'd make Keith bring the girl back. They'd find a way to heal her no matter what happened.

Lena pulled her hair into a ponytail and started gathering breakfast supplies. "Keith, don't stay away too long; we need information. And if Cole is moving east, Crystal is in danger. We have to find a way to warn them."

They hadn't wasted any time. It made sense to Evan, everybody was too far apart to sit around waiting till the time was perfect to do anything. And Newton Cole would never let them get away with it. Speed didn't help his throbbing arm; he could only be grateful that both wounds were on the same limb. At least he could fight. The doctor at Redstone had dressed his wound, and handed him a couple of joints, saying it was best he could do to get him ready to ride.

Riding hadn't been feasible after smoking a joint. So they'd hitched his horse along with one of theirs to a wagon that looked to be built for speed, not cargo. He was lying in the back, drifting a little, and well-padded; they'd be at the farm in half the time if they could keep up the pace.

The mayor had dispatched two people to get Evan home. Irv was one of them, the other was a woman Evan hadn't seen before. She'd obviously been in the battle; her face was scratched, and a patch of her blonde hair had been shaved so that a line of stitches could hold together the edges of the wound, and she had a finger cast on her left hand. Marley, Evan remembered now; Irv had introduced her before they put him in the wagon.

The dope was doing its job.

When he woke again, the sky was getting light. The pain in his arm had gone from a dull ache to a burning ache. He struggled to sit up, leaning against the side of the wagon. The horses had slowed to a walk. If he had his landmarks right, they had covered about a third of the distance while he'd been dozing. Irv and Marley had changed places on the bench; Marley was driving.

"The mayor said you could go right ahead and agree to an alliance?" Marley's words made Evan realize that they hadn't noticed him sit up.

"Not just go ahead and do it, it'll be a negotiation," Irv said.

Evan held the joint and matches in his good hand but decided not to light up and give away the fact that he was awake. Listening in might give him some information for Lena, or even for Prosperity.

"So, we're taking him back as a bargaining chip?" Marley flicked the reins and the horses sped up to a trot. "It seems like he might be their enemy just as much as he is ours. You can't trust people who change the town name to hide their past."

"That's a separate thing. The mayor told me not to make any promises about how we'll treat that place. She sent a couple of scouts over to check them out. Our job is the farm."

"Can't get there fast enough for me," Marley said, as she urged the horses to full speed again. "I'll be happy when I'm back home behind our walls."

Evan gritted his teeth against the jarring of the wagon. The vibrations were waking the pain in his hand and arm. He wouldn't be able to put off smoking the second joint for long.

"I heard what you suggested," Irv said, his voice loud enough to be heard over the horses and the creaks of the wagon. "You know he saved my life? He fought alongside us for Redstone. He can't be all that bad."

"You know where he comes from. My Joshua died because of them. The mayor thinks it's a bad idea to deliver his body back to the farm, something about it being irreversible. I reckon we could have said it happened when the Fort attacked."

"Kinda sounds like something that Abigail over in the Community of Hope would've said. We are all sorry about Joshua. What they did wasn't right. But always going after revenge doesn't seem to be a way for a healthy future."

Evan lit the joint, taking care to make sure the match was out before he tossed it over the side. He was grateful that the mayor and Irv had cooler heads. At least he could sleep on the journey without wondering if Marley would kill him regardless of orders.

CHAPTER TWENTY-SEVEN

Pallavi wiggled her fingers. The ropes around her wrists was still tight and her fingers were starting to swell.

She was mad at herself. When she'd found the road, she forgot to be careful. Of course, if the road was in such good shape somebody else would be taking it. All she had thought about was how quickly she would find a town on this stretch. How soon she would be able to get back to her dad. She didn't know how long the men had been watching her; they came out of the first piece of cover, so maybe they'd noticed her coming out of the trees.

No matter how much she'd struggled, they managed to get her across a horse. Not long after they'd stopped and tied her hands and feet, trussing her and throwing her back on the horse like a sack of flour. The blood rushed to her head and she passed out.

They'd made camp before she regained consciousness. But the sun was starting to come up now, and it had been pitch-dark the last she remembered. So maybe they'd traveled a couple of hours. They'd been camped long enough to set a fire and cook some meat. She could smell it; her stomach growled.

She knew these people were from the Fort. They were

stupidly arrogant, with such a big fire. If anyone was willing to take them on or was hunting them, they would give away their position. She didn't know if there were any wolves in the area, but maybe they were risking wild animals coming for the heat. But they didn't care, or maybe the animals were more afraid of the fire than she thought.

"She's awake."

The men were sitting across the fire from her, where both could see her. The two men looked so similar that she identified them in her mind as plaid shirt, and dirty yellow bandanna.

"How you doing, darlin'?" Plaid shirt asked.

Pallavi didn't speak. They hadn't gagged her, and she didn't want to risk that dirty bandanna being jammed in her mouth if she didn't say what they wanted.

The men laughed. Yellow bandanna stood and walked a few steps toward her. He held a tin cup out towards her. "It's just water. We need to keep you healthy. Cole won't want no damaged goods."

Pallavi looked down at her hands where blood was dried on her wrists.

"That'll heal. Ain't what I meant, anyway." He shoved the water towards her. Pallavi gulped half the cup in one go. "Don't you try to get away. We got to hang on to you for a few days. Got a mission. Then we all go back to the Fort."

Pallavi could imagine what that meant. She wouldn't let herself think about it. That was in the future. But if they had to keep her on the road with them for a few days that meant there would be opportunities to escape. They couldn't watch her all the time. They'd have to let her free to go to the bathroom. And they'd have to feed her at some point. But she wasn't going to ask. She wasn't going to be stupid again.

. . .

Scott finished cleaning his travel pack. Dust did a lot of damage to the leather, and he'd rather be prepared than delayed preparing his tack if he had to travel. Evan should have been back before him, not long before, but there was no way he could be this late. Scott gave Starbuck a pat as he passed the stall on his way to the kitchen. "Don't get too comfortable, pal. I got somebody to find."

He knew Lena would be in the kitchen. By now, the dishes from lunch would be put away and she'd be fixing something, maybe patching a shirt, or braiding new laces for a pair of boots. There was always something breaking down.

He opened the back door and saw her sitting at the table, a ball of wool spinning on the floor as she knitted what looked like a scarf. "We need to talk."

She chuckled. "Not that long ago I'd be worried you want to break up with me. There's so many more things these days that we need to talk about. I guess you mean Evan?"

Scott filled the glass of water from the tap, noticing the flow was a little low. When he got back he'd figure out what was wrong with the pump. "I should never have left him."

Lena continued knitting, her eyes on the needles as she spoke. "Keith's already looking for this Pallavi girl. Evan's not a kid; he probably just went back to The Community of Hope. From what you say, there was no news to bring anyway."

"Don't be pessimistic, they didn't say no. They said they wouldn't talk to anyone but you. And Evan wouldn't run off."

"We don't know him well enough to know either way. We're running out of time. If I'm going to send somebody else off, it should be me going to Redstone. Not someone else going to find a man who can take care of himself." She sighed and placed her knitting to the side. "Everything is taking too long, you know that. It's bad enough we don't have fast transport, or communication between the communities; if we can't form an alliance, how are we going to work on a plan to defend against anyone from the Fort?"

Scott put his glass in the sink. He joined Lena at the table, taking her hand. "We can't force it. And I can't leave Evan out there if he's hurt. What if his hand got worse? What if it's infected? It won't take me long, I can be back by the time you've figured out whether you're going to Redstone or not."

"I'm not going to Redstone. There are more of them, they can come here. If I go out on the road there'll be hardly anybody left here to defend the farm. I don't want to come back to find Newton Cole's men in place, and everybody dead, or being worked to death." She pulled her hand away. "We should be figuring out how to defend the farm ourselves. Evan said they were getting ready for some kind of attack. How long before they start killing?"

Scott felt the same frustration. Newton Cole was definitely sending scouts out, and, according to Evan, he was adding to his army. Without an alliance, the farm was lost anyway. Turning away from potential help was only going to get everyone killed. "If Cole takes the farm, and I don't know how we would stop him, then he'll control the traffic between Crystal and Redstone. He'll just pick them off once they are isolated. It's going to take him some time. I don't know for sure, but maybe we have four or five days. That's enough time to get reinforcements, but not enough time to get ready to take on those overwhelming odds."

"Is that supposed to cheer me up?" Lena smiled, and took his hand again. "I'm sorry, Scott. I do kind of feel bad for Evan. We just can't spare anyone right now. Maybe if Keith comes back with some news... No. What kind of news could he have that would give us time and resources to search for Evan, train for war, and solidify alliances with our neighbors?"

"So, are you saying no? As in, I'm not going to ask the others to weigh in. You're just making the decision?" He heard it in his voice as the words came out of his mouth, and he knew better. That kind of question was going to get Lena's back up.

Lena snatched her hand back. "Everyone's always expecting me to make decisions, and when I do, and you don't like it, that's how you react?" She stood, withdrawing from him physically and emotionally. "Yes. I meant no. And I'm not going to ask the others. We are in a crisis; we look after our own."

CHAPTER TWENTY-EIGHT

Scott sat alone in the kitchen trying to absorb what had just happened. He'd never seen Lena like this. They'd argued before, but it had always been a heated exchange. This time she'd shut him down. Lena hadn't wanted to be the leader, she'd fought it every day until they came to the decision that everyone would have a voice. And now, suddenly, only Lena had a voice.

He couldn't just leave Evan out there. If he tried to argue with Lena to get her to agree with his side, it would just take too long. Lena was stubborn, that was for sure; she didn't change her mind fast. And in this case she might not even listen to him; that hurt. It was probably better that they not talk about it now anyway, his gut was burning because of the way she'd spoken to him. All he could do was swallow the resentment and store up his arguments for what was going to be an epic fight when he got back. He pushed himself up from the table. He wasn't going to do as she told him, and not just because he felt responsible for Evan — because he didn't like to be told what to do.

Back in the barn, he started pulling together Starbuck's tack. He placed a bag of feed next to the saddle. If something had gone wrong, Evan's horse might be hungry. They kept stacks of trail food in the cupboard at the back of the barn. He stuffed a handful of the bars in another sack, checked the ammunition in his saddlebag, and picked up his rifle and bedroll. Scott took everything into the horse's stall and started saddling him.

"It's okay," he said as he patted Starbuck's flank. He'd gotten in the habit of talking to the animal when they'd traveled alone. "She will forgive us — eventually. When we've done this, we'll head out on a foraging trip, find some new supplies, maybe a present."

Starbuck whinnied back. He always agreed with Scott.

Scott packed everything on the horse, and then led him out of the stall. "I should've thought to get some meds, but I can't go back in the house. We have to get away before someone tries to talk me out of it."

"I came to say I was sorry." Lena was standing halfway between the house and the barn, watching Scott lead his horse toward the road. She tried not to let her anger take over again. "It looks like it doesn't matter to you what I want."

Scott and Starbuck came to a halt, but he didn't turn around right away. Lena wondered exactly what he was trying to deal with before facing her. Anger she could understand, or disappointment in her behavior, but if he said he was leaving forever, she didn't know how she'd feel. She didn't speak, afraid that she'd just make everything worse.

Scott's body relaxed and then he turned to face her. "You know you matter to me. Don't pretend otherwise. But I'm not going to leave him there. He was hurt, Cole's men are hunting, and he was out there doing something for us."

The kernel of fear in Lena's gut grew and twisted. Everything was supposed to be better here, but it was all falling apart. This is exactly why she didn't want to be the leader. Making unpopular decisions turned friends and lovers away. "I know all that. And those are all the same reasons why you shouldn't leave. You and Keith, and Tik, you're the ones with the best chance of protecting us if there's an attack. I know we can all shoot, but you're the best. Keith's gone. If you go, that leaves Tik and a bunch of people who think they're better shots than they are. I don't know if I can pull the trigger when it's a human being in my sight."

Scott took a step toward her, Lena took a step back. She wasn't ready for him to hug her and make everything better.

"I won't be gone long. The reasons you're giving are the same reasons we should get Evan. Whatever we think about Abigail, the men she sent to protect the road were trained. Remember? There was no doubt in my mind that if we had tried to run through them that first day, they would've shot us."

He was right, Lena knew that. But she was right, too. There was no easy choice. "How long will you be gone?"

"No more than two days. If I don't find him, or evidence that he's okay, I'll head back tomorrow."

The fear inside Lena subsided just a little. The anger she felt was mostly fear that he wouldn't come back. She said the only safe thing that she could. "Be careful."

Scott nodded.

The sound of horses galloping cut off whatever he was going to say. Scott raised his rifle and aimed towards the sound. Lena stood beside him, wishing she'd thought to bring her own weapon.

A dust cloud appeared at the rise in the road. A horse and wagon rushed through, the wagon driver pulling on the rains to slow the horses at the gate. "Looking for Lena," the driver yelled.

"Why?" Lena asked.

The passenger reached back into the bed of the wagon and dragged something up. It was Evan. He looked like death warmed over.

Scott lowered his rifle and stepped forward to help them bring Evan out, half carrying him into the house. In the kitchen, Lena called for Deb. Evan had come back with more injuries, although it looked like someone had tended him.

She stepped toward the man who'd spoken earlier. "Who are you? What happened?"

The man wiped the dust and sweat from his face, then dried his hands on the butt of his jeans. He held out his hand. "Name's Irv. From Redstone. Brought back your boy, ready to talk about teaming up."

Deb ran into the room, Maya and Jason right behind her. Lena sent Maya to deal with the horses and the wagon and turned her attention back to Irv. Lena shook his hand. "You found Lena. Get cleaned up, Jason will show you where. We will talk at dinner." When the strangers had left, following Jason upstairs, Lena pulled one of the chairs away from the table and sank into it. Finally, something was going right.

Evan sat in the back of the room while everyone else talked. He was trying to clear his head, but the dope Redstone had given him was potent. He was happy to let them argue it out.

"We have to move fast," Irv said. "You should send the kids back with us to Redstone. How many armed men and women do you need? How many guns do you have?"

Lena held her hands up for quiet. "We are not committing to anything until we've figured out a lot more of the picture. We're all important to defend. The main road passes close to all of us. It connects the country, and people are going to start using it. All the traffic from the east is going to pass through Prosperity. Anyone coming from the west is going to come to Crystal first. People are still coming up from the south, you guys know that in Redstone. We can't let Newton Cole control any of that."

Evan blinked, and pinched his leg to stay awake. He didn't see anybody getting ready to argue with Lena's description of the strategic position.

"And you are in the center of everything." Irv looked at his companion from Redstone. "You know we're not just talking about defense, right? Sooner or later, were going to have to take Cole out."

Evan watched that truth dawn on some of the faces in the room. He hadn't imagined they would think that Cole would stop at a little resistance. With everything that had happened, it was hard to remember that these were teachers and shopkeepers.

Tik put his arm around Mellow, who was sitting next to him at the table. "Cole's not going to let go until he has what he wants, or he's dead. He's just a gang leader. But we are not ready to go on the attack. We all need the alliances. Crystal needs a little persuasion, that's all."

"As far as we know, Cole hasn't touched Crystal yet." Lena pulled her hair back from her face. Evan could see the exhaustion in the little lines around her eyes. "We reached out to them, but they don't seem very interested. What if you went along? Explain what it's like being attacked. With your walls, I guess most of us figured you'd be the last that Cole would hit. It sends a potent message about the need to fight together."

"So, you're holding out on agreement with Redstone until the Council at Crystal agrees?" Marley stood and reached for her jacket. "I think we should head back, Irv."

Irv shook his head and motioned for her to sit. "There's some sense to it." When Marley was sitting, Irv turned his attention back to Lena. "What about Prosperity?" He nodded toward Evan. "When do they get brought in?"

They all turned to look at Evan. He tried to sit up and form complete sentences. "We're a little farther away from the Fort. We can wait until you guys have made your agreement. I could stay here and help, if you'll have me." He held up his injured hand. "If I'm of any use."

No one spoke for a moment. Evan was losing the battle with sleep in the quiet room.

"Let's say we agreed to go to Crystal," Marley said. "Who's coming with us?"

Relieved to have the room's attention off him, Evan leaned back against the wall. He needed rest; a couple of hours sleep, and he'd be fine.

"Keith's heading that way," Deb said. "Maybe you can meet up with him on the way there."

Evan opened his eyes. Why, when it was clear Cole was getting ready for something, had they sent their best fighter away?

"He has to find Pallavi," Maya said. "I don't know what Mahir would do if he thought we weren't looking for her."

There was a story here that Evan needed to figure out. The fuzziness in his brain was starting to lift, and his hand was starting to hurt again, but he wasn't ready to ask about Keith.

"By the time we meet up with him, he'll have her." Deb glanced above her head. "Let's not tell the boy anything other than that."

Maya looked like she was going to argue but a glance from her mother shut her up.

"It should be Lena," Scott said. "She didn't go to Redstone, and that caused problems. I don't think we can risk it again."

"They've already met me, it didn't seem to make a difference. It should be you, Scott, and Ava. And if you can pick up Keith on the way, three should be enough. It leaves us vulnerable. And you'll be gone a few days, but we should be okay."

The reality of the situation cleared Evan's mind a little. The farm couldn't really afford to send anyone, but here they were trying to organize the whole thing. At Prosperity, they thought they knew what was going on. This little group of people at the farm had figured it out long before.

Evan stood, weaving a little at the rush of blood to his head. He leaned against the wall to avoid falling. "I'll go. I know I'm not part of the farm, but I've seen this from every angle. Lena should come, too."

Lena opened her mouth to speak. Evan knew she was going to try and dodge it again. He shook his head. "We're just wasting time. Lena, you need to come because you make the final decision, no matter how much of a collective this farm is, you can speak for everyone. It'll be me and you, Irv and Marley, and if we find Keith we'll bring him with us. We could leave tonight. We are a big enough group, and we can be well armed. Cole and his men will avoid us." The last seemed to tumble out of his mouth in an effort to stop her arguing. It worked Lena just nodded and started telling people what to do in her absence.

CHAPTER TWENTY-NINE

The journey to Crystal had been a blur of pain for Evan. Lena had refused to allow Irv and Marley to take the wagon. So Evan had to forgo painkillers, or risk falling off his horse. They'd only rested for a few minutes every couple of hours. When they arrived, Irv had slipped him another joint. He smoked half of it while everyone was getting organized. Now the throbbing in his hand was calming down, and he could raise his arm a little. Unfortunately, his brain was getting fuzzy and that wasn't going to help.

He'd agreed to sit back and keep quiet until Lena called on him to tell his story. He still wasn't quite sure why she needed him to tell it. Both Irv and Marley were there.

They were in the living room of a house. The building itself was large and sprawled over most of the lot. A porch ran around the whole front, and the walk was lined with hydrangeas in pinks and blues. It was not something Evan usually noticed, but the dope was making him observe things he would've normally glossed over. The people from Crystal sat in comfortable armchairs next to a fireplace. Lena, Irv, and Marley sat in kitchen chairs opposite. They hadn't seen Keith on their way in, so it was just the four of them.

A young girl brought a tray of drinks into the room, offering Evan a glass of water. He saw whiskey on the tray and wondered how she'd known he shouldn't be drinking alcohol.

"So, you've come to tell us your decision?" The guy speaking looked to be about sixty, full head of yellowed white hair, faded blue eyes, and skinny enough to look sick. The other two he remembered from early on. Moira the redhead, and Stephen.

Evan recalled the offer he'd listened to. Crystal was looking to annex the farm, not form an alliance. It didn't bode well for the future, if they kept up that attitude. Someone looking to expand their influence, even peacefully, was as bad as Newton Cole who was trying to take it by force.

"We don't have a lot of time," Lena said. "Things have changed. Cole is escalating. We brought these people here from Redstone; they know what it's like firsthand."

"This Newton Cole," Moira said. "We understand how he's a problem for you, but that doesn't affect an agreement between us."

Evan almost stood up, but remembered that Lena had a plan, and it didn't include him blurting out everything at the first provocation.

"You think Cole isn't your problem?" Marley asked. "You think he'll be satisfied with Redstone and the farm? He's coming for you. Don't think for a second you are safe; Redstone has walls and he didn't care. If we make an alliance now, all of us, we'll be strong enough to stop him. If we don't, you'll be facing us on the other side. 'Cause Cole's just going to get stronger, and if he takes us, we won't be able to refuse to fight."

The older man glanced around the room, his eyes meeting Evan's. "Are you from Redstone, too?"

"My name is Evan White, I don't think we've been introduced."

"Ben; my name's Ben Atherton. I'm the head of this council. I asked you a question, Evan."

Evan glanced at Lena, but she gave him no indication of what she wanted. "No, sir, I'm from Prosperity."

Moira leaned forward and whispered something in Ben's ear. The old man frowned. "That what you call yourself now?"

Even with the buzz, Evan knew what was happening. Whatever he said now was going to make the difference between them dismissing him or hearing what he had to say and acting. And this was where diplomatic skills would come into play. And he had none. "Yes. We have new leaders, we don't do what we did before. I've been talking to Lena about an alliance. Hoping Redstone will come along as well."

"Why would they?" Ben asked. "What makes them trust you?"

Evan wished he had some coffee, or anything to clear his head. He'd asked himself the same thing on the road from Prosperity to the farm. Prosperity was under no illusion that it would be easy, but they had no idea.

Evan sat straighter and cleared his throat. "You mean why would they ally with us? There's a threat against all of us. Do I worry that the alliance will fall apart when we've dealt with Cole? Yep, but the important thing is to get Cole out of the way. We can work on a peaceful agreement later."

No one looked convinced. Crystal thought they were safe; that was where he had to hit them, so they'd wake up. "I've traveled all over our little slice of the country. I've seen Cole's men scouting and I've fought them alongside Redstone. Irv or Marley can tell you what that was like."

He took a sip of water. "Have you been to Redstone?" He waited for a response. "They have walls. I guess they thought they were invincible. Guards on the road to keep out anyone they didn't like. Cole sent his men and they got in. They killed a few, they damaged a few more."

"So, walls don't always work." Moira's freckles stood out as her face paled even more.

Evan shrugged. "What do you have? The river can be crossed

easily. There are fords a few miles in either direction. Cole's men could attack before you knew they were close."

Ben patted Moira's hand. She pulled away and continued. "We're not going to tell you what our defenses are, Evan. You have a point, and we'll reinforce what's there. But it doesn't change the fact that the fort is a long way from here, and you are all closer than we are."

Is she delusional? "He wants the whole area. He wants to control anyone and anything that tries to cross the country. Taking us, all of us, will give him that. There's no easy passage north of here. He'll keep expanding, getting stronger with each victory."

"He's not Hannibal crossing the damn alps," Joseph said.

"Not yet," Evan said. *Why isn't anyone stepping in to help? Maybe this is another test.*

He took another sip of water to stall for time. The big threat wasn't working. "Are you missing anyone else? More boys?"

Joseph swallowed and then looked at Ben. "A couple. Teens run all the time. They usually come back when they realize they can't feed themselves."

Evan thought through the haze of pain and dope. "A couple of boys, missing the last week?" He described what he could remember of the kids he'd seen.

Joseph stood. "Hal and Mika Olson."

"Cole's got them."

Now he had a reaction. The three Redstone people crowded together and started whispering. Evan took the moment to look at Lena, trying to get her to take over. She gave a quick thumbs up and turned to observe the conversation.

A thumbs up? What was he supposed to have done right?

"Why do you think he's doing this?" Ben asked. "He can't possibly have enough supplies to feed all those people. We've heard the fort is populated with mostly men. Is he taking girls too?"

"He's creating child soldiers." Joseph stepped in while Evan was working out the answer. "We all learned so much about the world before. Most of us learned about benign things: new methods of doing our jobs, languages, skills, how cute cats and puppies can be. But people like Cole learned from what horrified us. He's making boy soldiers."

It got silent as everyone contemplated that. Evan thought Cole was recruiting, but Joseph was right, and creating boy soldiers was a whole new level. None of the boys would be able to escape. He'd drug them, he'd threaten them, and he'd give them rewards they didn't know how to handle.

"Well?" he finally said. "What more do you need to know?"

"Do you have any plans?" Ben asked, and then went to the door and called for food. "It's all good to talk about joining forces to defend ourselves, but there's a lot of distance between us. Almost four days from here to Redstone." He glanced at Evan. "A bit more to Prosperity."

Evan looked at Lena again, hoping she had ideas, but she returned his gaze. The people at the farm were putting a lot of faith in him. "There are ways to shorten the journey. It won't be easy, but you're forgetting the smallholders in between. I can't see them refusing help."

"And it's just as far for Cole," Lena said, finally coming to his rescue. "He might be in a good position to defend, but to take us he'll have to come down to us. He still doesn't have enough men to strike us all at the same time."

Someone knocked on the door. Joseph answered it and muttered something. Then he took a tray of sandwiches and fruit from the person outside. Evan's stomach growled. He took a sip of water to stop from reaching for food as the tray passed. It would be uncivilized to grab before it was offered.

When the tray was on the table, Ben invited them to take what they wanted. "Don't pretend you aren't in need of sustenance."

When the visitors were eating, Joseph took over the conversation. "It's a strategy problem, right? For him and for us. What do you know about this Newton Cole?"

Evan stuffed his sandwich into his mouth. Lena grinned at him and said, "He's ex-military. We don't know which country. If I had to guess, I'd say he was local, Canadian or U.S."

"That means he'll have some experience in strategy," Joseph said. "Good thing we have some of that too. I was in the Canadian Air Force, when there was enough fuel to fly."

That surprised Evan. He still saw Joseph as the perfect teacher. "U.S. Navy." He didn't think his time as a private contractor was a good thing to bring up.

"We think he'll come for Crystal right away."

"Why not Redstone?" Ben asked.

"We already pushed back. Like Evan said, they came at us, testing. We might be too much trouble."

Ben pulled the cork on a bottle of whiskey. "Time to drink to our relationship. Let's get down to the details."

As he poured, someone rapped on the door, entering without waiting for acknowledgment. A young woman, late teens, maybe early twenties at most. She was covered in grime and sweat. Her breath coming in gulps, she strode toward Ben. "A force is coming, maybe ten, twenty men. Heavily armed. They'll be here in a day at the latest."

CHAPTER THIRTY

The fuzziness cleared from Evan's head. There was no way Cole could have timed that, but still it felt as though he picked the best moment to do the worst damage.

Lena stood and faced the scout. "How heavily armed were they? Exactly where did you see them? Why can't you be more precise about the numbers?"

The scout was young, and given the attitude here, probably hadn't had much experience. Evan stepped closer to the girl. "Take a breath. We need to ask you some questions, so we can be ready." He waited until her breathing was under control. "What your name, scout?" The others started to crowd her, but Evan nudged them back. Stephen's military training kicked in, and he drew the mayor away. Evan heard him mumbling explanations.

"Lily. My name's Lily Youngston." She accepted the glass of water that Moira handed to her.

"Let's start with why you don't know how many there are. What makes you uncertain?" Evan knew taking the time to let the girl gather her thoughts would save them a lot of heartache later. To her credit, she pulled herself together as she drank the water.

"They're using the trees for cover. The next scout will have better information. We just figured you needed to know they were coming, and you could wait for the details."

At least their scouts knew how to prioritize. "Did you see anyone other than just the men?" Since he learned that Cole's men had taken a young girl, Evan had been worried. It was bad enough to turn young men into killing machines. But he was pretty sure Cole wasn't an equal opportunity kinda guy.

"No. But maybe they had a camp somewhere. They had rifles, and we saw them down by the exit to the highway." She held up the glass for a refill.

Lena stepped forward. "What makes you think it's going to take them a day? You got here faster than that, right?"

Lily nodded. "There's too many of them to come the way I came. And the other scouts are kinda harassing them. I don't know how long we'll be able to hold them off."

Evan thanked Lily and told her to get some rest. He turned to the group standing in front of the fire. There was no time to get reinforcements from anywhere, but it seemed like they hadn't just been sitting around relaxing in the comfort of knowing Cole was a long way away. The scouts were proof that they'd been preparing for battle.

He addressed Ben directly. "It's a lot of men, but I'm guessing you can rally some forces. We should probably figure out a few of those details right now, but just enough so we trust each other after the battle."

Ben turned to Lena, obviously thinking she was his peer, and Evan was just a soldier. "The boy's right, we've been training. Joseph here has overseen that. Will you fight beside us? At least for this battle?"

Lena held out her hand. "Let's shake on it. I'm sure someone here has some legal experience. But no matter what we put in an agreement, it's only going to be as good as our intentions to keep it. Is a handshake good enough for you?"

Ben laughed and shook her hand. "Stephen, take these folks and show them where they can get ready to fight."

Night had passed quickly in a rush of setting up teams of people to fight together. Joseph and Evan had worked side by side, at least after an initial disagreement. Somehow the rivalry between their different branches of the military survived even the destruction of the world.

Now, Evan stood beside Lena on the mayor's left side, Moira and Joseph were on his right. Irv and Marley were already deployed with a small group of people from Crystal. Despite their behavior in the past, Cole's men had asked for a parlay. Five of them sat on their horses blocking the road.

"You asked for a parlay," Ben said, his voice pitched to carry across the space. "Start talking."

"There's no need for anybody to be hurt." There had been no introductions. The man speaking was at the center of the line. "Just call off your people and let us in without a fight. I promise, Cole can be quite generous to his friends."

To his credit, Ben didn't laugh at the transparent offer. Evan observed him as he took his time in answering. Maybe if he paid attention to someone who knew how to play politics, he'd gain the skill.

"Is anyone taking you up on that offer?" Ben asked.

"Not my offer, old man." The spokesperson turned and growled something to his companions, who were laughing. "The offer comes from Cole. And he ain't offered it before."

Ben nodded like he was thinking it over. "Any idea why I'm honored this way?"

"I don't question Cole. He don't like it when people step up."

Evan was itching to shoot the smile off the guy's face. He knew that was uncivilized. And he knew if he did it, it would just reinforce what people thought of Prosperity. But some people just seemed to be asking for a little attitude straightening. The mayor was doing a good job of stalling. They knew when they stepped outside to meet these men there would be no just turning around and walking back. Evan wasn't even sure that if they agreed to the offer that they wouldn't get shot anyway. Leaving someone alive who can take over seemed like a poor strategy.

"Can we have some time to think it over?"

"All the time you need. That is if you only need right now."

It was pretty clear that Cole had only taught his men to be brutal and nothing about strategy. They were downhill, there was plenty of cover just past the edge of the road, and the sun was almost high enough to be in their eyes. Evan could see two of Crystal's fighting groups easing their way to the edge of the cover. What worried him was the fact that he couldn't see the rest of Cole's men.

"I've lived this long knowing that you don't make these kinds of decisions on a dime. You're welcome to wait there, we'll get back to you." As Ben turned away, his people fired simultaneously from behind the five men. They didn't kill anyone. But they scared the horses. And Cole's men had been reaching for their weapons, so they were caught by surprise.

"Get your asses back in town," Ben said, as he ran by. "It won't work for very long."

CHAPTER THIRTY-ONE

No matter how much she struggled, Pallavi couldn't get free. She hadn't thought beyond just getting her arms and legs loose from the ropes. When she had a chance to run, she'd go in whichever direction presented itself.

"We can't leave her here," the man who'd captured her said. "Not 'less we leave someone to watch her. And there ain't enough of us as we can spare one."

"God dammit, Ezra, bring her along then. She gets shot, it ain't me who has to tell Cole."

It didn't faze her captor. He grunted as he lifted her off the ground, swearing under his breath afterward. "You be still," he whispered in Pallavi's ear after he slung her over the back of the horse.

"Just tie me to one of the trees," Pallavi said. "I can't get away. If you take me with you, it's going to be hard for you to fight." She didn't expect him to do it, but she had to try.

"Not going to happen, honey. I'm going to keep you right by my side." He laughed. "At least right by my backside."

All Pallavi could do was try to stay on the horse. At least the man didn't kick her as he mounted it. She knew, because they kept reminding her at every opportunity, that Newton Cole wanted her unmarked.

She also knew, because they talked about it openly in front of her, everything they were planning to do. That might be useful information if she could get it to the people they were fighting.

"You think these townies are ready for us?" Ezra asked his partner. There were only the two of them. Pallavi knew there were other groups out there, but as far as she knew, everyone was scattered, not forming groups.

"Stop asking that. How the hell should I know?" The other man spat on the side of the road. "That's what we're here to learn. So's Cole can figure out who to hit first. Just don't get shot, don't get her damaged, and don't get distracted. We're in, we're out, and we're back at the fort."

The bouncing from the horse's gait jarred her. She tucked her face into the animal's flank to minimize the movement. It meant she didn't have as good a view of where they were going, but that wouldn't help if she ended up with broken teeth and a bitten off tongue.

Mahir would be worried by now. She hoped he wasn't looking for her. Maybe she should have been more patient; a couple of days would not have made any difference. But she'd been cocky, and now she was paying for it.

They had traveled downhill, but now the land was flattening out. The horse slowed and Pallavi realized she could hear other people around her.

"I think we should teach them a lesson." This was a new voice. A man; they all seemed to be men. "We can still get information. And Cole might be happy if we brought a few prisoners back. Maybe pretty ones like her, or a few more boys we can train."

"You want to punish them for your stupidity, Mike?" Ezra asked. "You shoulda expected them to fight back a bit. Are you only good if the other guy surrenders?"

Pallavi listened to the other men laugh. Was this normal? Or could she use the fact that they didn't respect each other to escape?

From what she'd heard of their plans, Pallavi knew they were getting ready to attack. She lifted her head as much as she could. They were in a small valley looking up at some buildings. She could see about ten men on horses with Ezra, but from the sounds of it there were a few more out of her sight. No one commented on the armed men and women she could see creeping up on them.

Crystal's readiness impressed the hell out of Evan. As they ran back from the confrontation, the residents handed out weapons. By the time he was behind cover, Evan had a rifle, a box of ammo, and a team of four fighters. If his wounds didn't hurt so damn much, he'd be eager for the fight.

Now they were waiting for the mayor to give them the go-ahead.

"I'm Evan," he said to his small team. "This isn't my first battle with these guys. What about you?"

His team was made up of three women and a man. He wanted to know what skill level he was working with.

"I'm Lucy," a redhead announced. Crystal seem to have more than its share of redheads. Lucy pointed at the man beside her. "That's Bill. Over there is Mary; I think you know Lily."

Evan hadn't noticed the scout he'd talked to. She'd used camouflage paint on her face, and her hair was hidden under a black wool hat. She grinned at him and he felt heat rise in his cheeks. "Good to meet you," he said. "So, I know Lily is a scout and she's seen these guys. What's your background, Lucy?"

"We are all trained, but none of us has been in a real fight." Lucy seemed comfortable speaking for everyone.

"Okay, when it starts, stay low, don't waste ammo, and stick close to me. It's all gonna happen real fast." Evan didn't have time to say anything else because the order to go was passed along. At least they had the sense not to yell. They needed as much surprise as they could get. If they were wrong about these guys just gathering information, it could turn into a slaughter.

Evan led his unit from behind the hedge following two other groups. The attackers were spread out again, giving Crystal's forces the advantage of the slope. The sun wasn't helping this time, and soon it would be in the defenders' eyes. "We'll get on their flank. Head for the trees; if we get separated we'll meet up there. Our job is to make sure they don't have a way out other than back up the road."

Evan let his team get ahead of him so that he could check out the opposition. They still hadn't noticed the people leaving Crystal. But it wouldn't be too long. He counted twelve men on horseback. They didn't seem to be waiting for anyone or checking to see if reinforcements were in place. Every single one of them had bags hanging from their saddles. These guys were ready to run for home. One of them had a girl strapped behind him. Probably this Pallavi. Evan concentrated on that man. If he couldn't get the girl away during the attack, he wanted to know which of them to follow.

As Evan slipped into place with his team, he heard a shout: Cole's men finally noticing they weren't alone. In seconds there were gunshots, horses screaming against their rider's instructions, and the chaos of a battle.

"Wait," he said. "We only shoot if they come this way. Let the others do some damage." Even for an experienced soldier, waiting his turn was hard. Evan watched his team closely; they held steady, rifles up, but no one looked like they were about to shoot out of fear or panic.

A horse threw his rider and ran towards Evan's position. At the last minute, he veered to avoid the trees. His rider hit the ground.

The rider scrambled to his feet, then, dodging the other

horses, retrieved his rifle. Then he backed away. Stopping to wait for his compatriots outside the action.

The man with the girl on his horse stayed to the outside of the skirmish. She was doing her best to upset his balance, to confuse the horse, and generally make him a liability rather than an asset.

One of the defenders hit an attacker. The man fell from his horse and didn't get up. That horse ran away, too.

"Are we going to get a chance?" Lily asked. "I don't want to sit out here watching the action."

"If we're lucky we'll just be spectators. These guys don't know what they're doing. Although, I guess it's possible they're trying to hustle us. But it doesn't make sense that they would risk losing men and horses to lull us into underestimating Cole."

Evan saw two of the defenders fall. One of them tried to crawl back into the town, but another bullet brought him to a stop. Then another attacker hit the ground. A shout from the man carrying the woman brought the attackers around and retreating in the direction of the fort.

"I could get one of them," Bill said, aiming.

Evan reached for the barrel of the rifle with his bad hand and pushed it down. The pain cut through the adrenaline and he swore. "No. You could hit the girl. Just be glad it wasn't worse."

CHAPTER THIRTY-TWO

Evan rode at the rear of the small group returning to the farm. After the fight, Lena wouldn't let him go after Pallavi. She said that Keith would find her, and it was more important to settle the alliance than run to the rescue.

The only good point she'd made, in his opinion, was that running after the attackers now might get in Keith's way.

He couldn't sit through another negotiation. His hand hurt, he was exhausted, and he didn't trust himself not to say the wrong thing. To say it at the top of his lungs and follow it up with a punch at the nearest person. Pain and a weed hangover was a bad combination. She must have seen it in his eyes, because Lena sent him off to rest while they talked.

At breakfast, Irv caught him up. Crystal was sending a few people to the farm. They'd spent most of the night trying to figure out where Cole would strike first — a real strike, not a testing of defenses. Everyone had their own idea, so eventually Crystal agreed to send weapons and ammo with Lena along with a few fighters. "Me and Marley will stay, too. The farm probably can't take in any more right now."

Evan's mood had not improved with sleep. Now they were a

couple of hours into the trip back. They were riding hard, but not as hard as when they came. The wagon full of supplies slowed them down. The sun was up, but clouds filled the sky, diffusing the light, and dampening the sound. It was probably going to rain.

"Cheer up," Irv said. He reined his horse to drop back and ride with Evan. "We'll get this done, and then the fun can begin."

"What fun?" Evan hung onto his mood.

"Well, alliances mean we'll be visiting more. There are women in Prosperity who need to meet me." He puffed up his chest.

"Oh," Evan said.

"I saw you checking out those redheads in Crystal. Don't blame you, they seem damn fine."

Evan grinned. "I bet they are, why would they stoop to look at me?"

"Don't they have mirrors in Prosperity?" Irv leaned closer. "You are a good-looking man. These are new times. Maybe monogamy is on its way out."

Marley turned in the saddle. "Keep it down. And don't go putting money on the monogamy thing. People are still territorial and if you wander, someone is going to get hurt." She nudged her horse to speed up.

"Did I miss something?" Evan had been stoned for most of the time he'd been with Irv and Marley.

"Yup, that's my wife." His admiration of Marley colored his earlier words in Evan's memory.

"I'd be scared to even joke about it," Evan said.

"Yeah, you get with one of those redheads and you'll know what scared means." Irv reached over and slapped Evan on the back. "Don't get so hung up on what's happening right now. There's always a future, Evan."

Evan grunted a response.

The riders ahead slowed to a stop. Evan was more than ready for a rest. The pain in his hand and arm was easing, and he needed to keep his mind clear, so another joint was out of the question. If he missed something more important than Irv's love life, it could mean disaster.

He joined the others to see Keith standing next to Lena's horse.

"No sign of her," Keith said. "I know I should have stayed, but Ava said you'd gone with no protection. I guess she exaggerated."

Evan dismounted and joined Keith at Lena's side. "I think the girl is with the men who attacked. They should be halfway back to the fort by now."

"You don't know that," Lena said. "I don't want to leave her either. Her brother is at the farm, and he expects us to save her. But we can't spare the men."

Keith hitched his pack higher on his shoulders. "One man won't make a difference, but if you leave that girl to Newton Cole, you'll regret it forever."

"I know, but—"

"Look, I can go," Evan said. Keith might eventually convince Lena, but Pallavi didn't have eventually. "I'm not going to be much use in a fight. If those guys had come at my unit, we'd be dead. I'll be more use going after her. Keith can go back with you."

Lena looked at him, then at Keith, then around at everything. She sighed. "Okay. I can't argue with you. If it was Maya or Mellow, or anyone I knew, I'd be all over the rescue. Be careful. We do need you."

"No, you don't," Evan said, looking at the men and women from Crystal. "You have plenty of help."

She leaned down and whispered, "And how will we ever convince the people in Prosperity that we didn't harm you? Plus, and don't tell anyone this, I've come to like you, Evan. So, don't get killed."

. . .

He'd found the raiding party's tracks leading toward the trail to the fort.

The entrance to the trail was muddied from the rain that finally hit. It was clear that Cole had multiple parties out gathering information. Evan hadn't thought of the smallholders in the area; they wouldn't have been able to repel a raid as easily.

He knew these were the men who'd attacked Crystal because they were the only tracks coming from that direction. Now he had a choice. Take the horse up the trail and risk him being stolen because there were only a few places to hobble him, or leave him here. There was still plenty of cover for the horse not that far from the trail. It would make the climb harder, but Evan could sneak better on foot.

He rode to a small clearing. The river was shallow there and the grass still thick. "I won't hobble you," Evan whispered. "Just don't run away unless they come for you."

The horse whinnied and started cropping the grass.

Evan knew the animal would stay and eat for a while. As long as nothing spooked him, the horse would be here in a couple of hours.

The sun set as Evan crested the rise. His old vantage point was still his best bet to see what was happening. He needed intelligence before making a plan.

The Fort was bright again. When they took Cole down, someone would have to find out how he managed to create electricity to power all of it.

Evan lay on his stomach, placing his rifle beside him, and stared at the action below.

Cole was in the courtyard again. Three of his men were talking to him, probably reporting. One of them Evan recognized from the raid on Crystal. Across the courtyard, outside what looked like stables, there was a line of men, and a few boys. They were taking turns looking in a small grated window. The ones behind jostling for their turn.

Ugly laughs echoed from the crowd. Evan couldn't make out the words, but he could see the gestures. Pallavi — or if not her, some other woman, was inside. They were tormenting her. Softening her up for Cole?

Pallavi cowered in the corner of the room. It was dark and smelled of horses, although, after the last two days, everything smelled of horse. They'd ridden past the walls of the Fort and she'd been manhandled into the room, tripping over a saddle and almost falling on a stack of spurs.

Men were leering at her and saying horrible things. Even in the darkest corner, she couldn't get away from them. No matter what she tried, there seemed to be no way to escape. Not on the road, not from here, not from whatever they planned to do with her.

"Yeah, I'd be willing to do Cole's bidding to get her when he's done," a rough voice said. The man banged on the wall. Pallavi felt the vibrations even in the back of the structure.

"You'll be behind me in the lineup," another harsh voice answered. "Hey, sweet thing, you be nice and maybe you'll live a long time."

Why are they doing this?

Pallavi thought she understood how men could be rough and uncivilized. She didn't understand why they were being so cruel. Was it better for them if her spirit was broken before they had their fun? Or did they think this was courtship. If her father was here... The thought caused more pain than anything these men did. She knew, in her heart, that no miracle had come to save her dad. That she'd left Mahir alone on the pretense of finding help. It was cowardice. If she really wanted help, she'd have gone to the farm. Tears burned, she wiped them away and straightened. She would escape and go home.

More banging on the walls, and dirt sifted down from the ceiling. If it was her only option, perhaps she could dismantle the room.

How do I do that without it collapsing on me?

Suddenly the catcalling and banging stopped. The only sound was feet shuffling away from the wall. Pallavi's heart thudded in her chest. If they left her alone, even for a few minutes, she'd find a weakness.

The lock rattled, and the door opened. Whoever it was had a lantern. She covered her eyes with her arm to protect her sight.

"Don't be so coy, darlin'."

The brightness receded. Pallavi braved a glance.

The man standing inside the door was tall and white, and he was smiling. His dark hair was combed back, and he'd shaved. She knew he thought the smile would disarm her, make her feel safe. All she felt was her skin crawling. There was no warmth in his eyes. She was being assessed as an asset, not a person.

"Let me go," she said. In her head, it sounded brave and regal; by the time the words came out they were cracked and frightened.

"Oh, now that would be a shame," he said, taking a step forward.

Pallavi had nowhere to go. The boards wouldn't yield.

"Be nice, and we'll be nice back," he said.

"Who are you?" Pallavi could see through the open door. There was no one outside. Could she get past him?

"You know who I am. Newton Cole." He gestured to the outside. "This is my place."

Pallavi closed her eyes.

"You'll be let out of here tonight," Cole said. "You can have a bath, a hot meal."

She gathered her bravery. "When?" The single word came out strong. "How long do I have to put up with the disrespect?" It wasn't the word she wanted to say but antagonizing this man would not get her free.

"I'll make sure no one bothers you," Cole said.

"Why can't I come now?" When they moved her, maybe she could run?

"You need a little attitude adjustment. A taste of what it's like to be on my bad side," Cole said the words gently.

At least it would be quiet for a while.

CHAPTER THIRTY-THREE

Evan waited until quiet settled over the Fort. He'd watched Cole visit the stable. Lying there looking down on the action, he wanted desperately to run in and rescue the captive. But that would only get him captured. So he watched while Cole's men got drunk, some slowly, some fast enough to convince him they'd been halfway there all day. Now it was full dark, and if he was going to make his move it had to be now.

The last time he'd been here, he hadn't been looking for a way in. Now, he noticed the garbage pile was higher than it had been before, and there was a building just inside the walls. With luck, the trash wouldn't collapse underneath him, and he'd be able to launch himself onto the roof of the building without more injury. As far as he could tell, it was used for storage, and no one was inside.

The approach to the fort was unguarded, at least from the side he could see.

He made it to the garbage heap, scrambling to the top and crouching beside the wall without hurting himself. From this vantage point, the plan didn't look so perfect. He was going to have to climb three feet of wall, and then balance on the narrow top before making the leap. He hadn't been able to see what was on the ground. He'd have to make that decision when he was at the top of the wall. The only thing he knew was it was a long way down. He steeled himself before making the move. It was going to have to be fast, because he couldn't perch up there for more than a second.

Evan sprang at the wall, scrambling to the top. Raising his legs, he glanced down to see empty barrels below him. He shifted his weight so that his momentum would take him to the roof of the building as originally planned.

He landed as quietly as he could, but in his ears it sounded as loud as a cannon shot. No one paid attention. The stable was halfway along the wall from where he stood. No convenient rooftops for him to hop across.

"Why you think Cole's been so generous with the booze?"

Evan froze. There were at least two men below him.

"I don't ask questions when he's handing stuff out. Just enjoy it and hope he stays in a generous mood."

Evan lay on his belly and looked down. Two men were leaning against the side of the building, he'd missed them in the shadows. One of them lit a cigarette. There weren't that many of those around.

Of course, this side was the most direct route to his goal. Evan couldn't wait until they moved on; every second he spent up on this roof was another second for somebody to look up and see him.

He moved away, holding his breath as he crossed to the other edge. This time there was no one in sight. He turned and dropped his legs over the edge of the roof, letting himself slide to the ground, bending his knees and rolling as he hit. He moved into the shadows, waiting for a reaction.

Nothing happened.

The men were all too drunk, or too stoned, to pay attention to the little noises of the night. Rather than worry about it,

Evan decided he take the man's advice: just enjoy it and hope it lasted.

He couldn't risk going to the small window and looking inside. His only option was to lean against the side wall, pretending to be one of Cole's men. It was too dark to make out any details. He felt the rough boards, hoping for a crack. His fingers found a knothole. "You okay?" He didn't whisper but kept his voice as low as he could.

Pallavi stopped digging. The fact that Cole's men were sloppy with their equipment had left her a lot of options for tools. Unfortunately, the dirt was too hard-packed for her to have made more than a dent.

She sat back, fighting despair. There was no point in giving up now. She had nothing better to do; it would just be nice to have made some progress. She heard scratching, it was too far from the ground to be rats. And then a voice. "You okay?"

Had Cole lied when he told her he'd called his men off? Was this a new torture, or a test to see if she was compliant?

"No. How could I be?"

"Yes, sorry. Are you hurt? I mean, badly enough that you can't run?"

Pallavi's whole body ached. "No. Can you get me out?"

"I'm gonna try. Are you tied up?"

At least it wasn't one of the men who was leering at her earlier. "No."

"Okay. Get to the door."

Was he just going to walk her out of here?

"Then what?" She wasn't going to do as he said until she had as much information as she could get out of the man. When she walked away from the wall they wouldn't be able to communicate.

"I'm not sure. There's lots of places to hide, and there's hardly anybody out here. We'll figure our next step once you're out."

Pallavi tried to think of the consequences of this being a trick. If some of his men had decided to defy Cole's orders, leaving here could be walking into a gang rape. But this man didn't seem to know what had happened to her up to now. He'd asked if she was hurt, but all of Cole's men had seen her when she arrived. He'd asked if she was tied up, but surely everyone who looked in that window had passed on the news that she wasn't.

A few minutes ago, all she wanted was out of this room. She hadn't had a plan either. "I'm going to the door."

Evan didn't have time to feel relieved that she hadn't made it harder. Before he stepped into full view, he peered around the corner, taking in the courtyard and paying attention to the shadows. He did not want to get surprised again. The noise coming from the main house was getting louder. Cole's men were getting drunker.

He walked to the door as if he had every right to do so. Even without anybody watching, he didn't want to sneak and tip off the fact that he didn't belong there. On the outside, it was a simple padlock. He slid his travel knife out of his boot, jammed the handle into the padlock shank, twisted and caught the lock as it popped out. He tugged at the door until it was wide enough for the girl to slip out. He pointed to where he been standing earlier and followed her there.

She was dirty, but who wouldn't be after what she'd been through? Her dark hair was a mass of tangles. And her eyes were enormous. She didn't look frightened, which was a good thing in the circumstances. She looked angry.

"Are you Pallavi?"

"How do you know my name?" She looked around as though planning her own escape.

"Your brother sent us after you. I'll tell you more when we're out of here." He leaned around the corner of the building, to ensure that no one had left the party. "Did you notice anything when they brought you in?"

"I was hung over the back of a horse."

"I don't think it's a good idea if we go out the front door, anyway. Before we go, I want to do a little reconnaissance. These guys are going to attack, and if we can find out when we can get more prepared."

"You go ahead, I'll figure out how to get out of here by myself." She moved away from Evan and into the shadows of the wall.

He reached out and drew her back, grateful that she didn't make any noise in protest. "You won't get out by yourself. Stay here. I'll be back in just a few minutes."

"No, I'm sticking with you. If something happens it's better if there are two of us." She nodded toward the house. "You're going there, right? I can watch your back."

"Are you sure? You were just about to run off by yourself."

"Yeah. I'm gonna need you to boost me up to the top of the wall anyway."

Evan told her to stay close behind him; he might be able to pass for one of Cole's men, but she was a target. Now, instead of walking confidently up to the window, he had to sneak around. They hugged the shadows until they had no choice but to move out into the light. "We need to do this fast," he said. "Fix your eyes on that window." He pointed to an open window on the side of the house. There was some convenient shadow to the other side of it. And he could occasionally see someone's shoulder as they walked past. "Don't run, it calls attention to you. But don't dawdle."

He scanned the area one more time before giving her the nod to go. He held his breath, but no one noticed her. As soon as she was settled, he strode over to join her. As long as their luck held, Evan was planning to ride it.

He blushed as they listened to Cole's men talk. It was mostly about Pallavi, and what they expected her night to end with.

Over the few minutes that he was willing to risk, Evan learned that the bar was open all night, that Cole wasn't usually that generous, and that his men weren't as respectful when they'd been drinking. Nothing that would help them figure out where the attack was coming. Beside him, Pallavi was trembling. He couldn't keep her here much longer and expect her to be able to climb out. Evan wasn't sure if he was able to do it himself.

He tapped her on the arm, and nodded back to where they had come from, not willing to have a conversation so close to all the men in the house.

She'd barely taken a step when the conversation changed in the house. Someone important had come into the room. Evan put a hand on her arm to stay her.

"Where the fuck is Ray?" That could only be Cole.

"Right here, Boss." This voice was sober.

"Are they going to be ready?"

"They'd be a lot more ready if you close the bar," Ray said. "Any more booze, and they won't recover enough to get two days prep in because they'll still be passed out at noon tomorrow. You want them fighting at the farm two days after that, you cut off the booze from now until after we win."

If they closed the bar now the men would start coming from the house and their chances of escape would drop from slim to none. Evan couldn't see anybody standing directly in front of the window, but it was a risk to move now. It was an even bigger risk to wait. He scanned the area, this time looking behind the house. There was a garden with a wall separating the compound from Cole's private space.

Evan pointed, thinking they would be better with the boost from that wall to the outside. And it was dark enough back there that no one would see them. It seemed the back of the house was party free.

He boosted Pallavi up, and then accepted her hand even though she was too weak to help him. It wouldn't take more than a running jump to grab the top of the outside wall, but he had no idea what was out there. "Do you think you can jump?" he asked Pallavi. She nodded without even looking at the wall. "I'm gonna go first, so if you don't think you can get there you need to say so now."

"I can do it," she said. "If you go first, how are you going to tell me what to do?"

"If you don't hear anything, come running, I'll help you land. If I fall and hurt myself, I'll scream loud enough that you'll know. If that happens, find some place to hide. They'll be too busy looking for me, you'll be able to sneak out the front door. Get to the farm."

"Okay, enough talking."

"Who the fuck are you?" Someone had come into the backyard.

CHAPTER THIRTY-FOUR

Pallavi hugged the side of the outer wall. She needed Evan to boost her up and he was moving toward the man. She didn't recognize him from her tormentors, but they had been so brutal the faces blurred together.

She covered her mouth with her free hand, pressing tight to keep the screams from flying out.

Evan reached the man before another word got out. She watched as he punched him in the temple and then caught him as he fell. Then Evan pulled a knife out of his boot. Suddenly there was a spray of blood painting the back of the house.

Evan wiped the blade on the ground and ran back to Pallavi. He reached for her and she almost lost her footing as her body instinctively drew back.

"You have to let me past," he whispered. "We need to go now."

She knew it was a reality, brutal and swift death, but it was the first time she'd seen someone do it, and Evan didn't seem even a little affected.

"Are you going to be sick?" he asked.

She shook her head, even though the back of her throat was burning to vomit. She swallowed and moved aside.

"Can you give me a boost?" Evan asked. "We don't have time to wait for me to scramble up and then drop first. I can reach the top, but I need a little push."

She bent and laced her fingers together. He placed his boot in her hands.

"On three, I'll pull, and you push as hard as you can. Then be ready for me to pull you up."

Pallavi nodded. If she spoke, the screams and vomit would escape.

"One, two, three."

Pallavi pushed, but Evan gave most of the effort. She reached up as soon as his boot was out of her hands. Evan was poised on the edge of the wall. He reached for her.

"Jump. There's a soft landing, but bend your knees and roll."

She walked back along the wall, then ran toward his outstretched hand.

Pallavi jumped.

Their hands connected.

She vaulted the wall, tucking her legs under so she landed with knees bent.

The force knocked the wind out of her, but she rolled, and scrambled to her feet as she heard Evan hit the ground.

"We need to get around the wall to the other side. I have a horse at the bottom of the trail. Can you run?"

Pallavi didn't bother answering, just ran in the direction he pointed.

She didn't stop when they reached the top of the trail. She careened down the dark path, not caring if she fell. She arrived at the bottom, out of breath, feeling sick for a new reason, knees and elbow skinned from the few stumbles. But she was away from the danger of the Fort.

Evan joined her and they both gasped for breath. Pallavi ran to the closest bush and emptied her stomach contents; mostly bile.

"That man," she said, when her body stopped heaving. "You..." she couldn't finish the sentence.

Evan nodded his head toward a clearing. "If I hadn't done it, he would have called out."

"I know," Pallavi said, following him. "It's just... Don't you feel bad? I mean, yes he deserved it, but..."

Evan stopped. "I can't get sentimental right now. At any moment, someone's going to notice you're gone. That's if they don't find this body first. I'll feel bad about what happened when we are safe and the people at the farm are ready to face Cole's men when they come."

The trek to and from Redstone was grueling. Lena was glad to see the farm lit and welcoming.

A seat that didn't move underneath her, even a hard kitchen chair, was going to feel like heaven. "Leave the horses at the stable," she said to the rest of the group. "I'll send someone down to take care of them. I think we've earned a drink and a rest." No one complained.

As they walked up the steps, Ava opened the door. "Welcome back. Are we celebrating, or drowning our sorrows?"

It was hard to agree to celebrate with everything that was hanging over their heads, but Lena knew she couldn't solve all her problems at once. "Is Evan back?" she asked, stalling for time.

"He's not with you?"

Keith trudged past. "He went after the girl. He saw her just outside Crystal. I need a bath."

Lena introduced the rest of the team as they entered the house. "We need to find them a place to bunk down," she said.

"So, what do we tell Mahir?" Ava asked. "He's barely sleeping he's so worried. There's not much of him to start with, I'm worried he's going to fade away to nothing."

Lena headed for the kitchen. Whatever happened next, she

needed a glass of water that didn't taste like the container. "Is he in bed now?"

Ava nodded. "I don't know if he'll come down. He's pretty shy, so we might be able to put off an answer until morning."

Lena glanced around at the stairwell, it looked like she wasn't going to get her reprieve. Mahir was sitting on the top step. She detoured to the bottom of the stairs and beckoned him down. "Evan will find her, it won't be long now." She hated lying, but the kid needed some hope.

He didn't smile in response, or even speak. Mahir just turned away and walked back to his perch at the top of the stairs.

"I know it's late," Lena said. "But the horses need tending to, and we need to give everybody an update. And it would be great if you could make us something to eat. I'm not sure I'll survive another trip like that. My old body can't handle two all day rides."

"You guys get cleaned up," Ava said in her take-charge voice. "I'll see to the horses. And I'll get some food going; you can update us in, say, an hour?"

The others were already rousing, Lena took her glass of water as she passed the tap, Ava bent and encouraged Mahir to come downstairs.

Thank God her aunt had installed enough bathrooms for each bedroom. She directed visitors where to clean up and told them to head for the dining room when they were done, knowing Ava would have tea and snacks on the table before anyone entered.

Dressed in clean clothes, hair wet from the tepid shower, and surprisingly refreshed, Lena walked into the dining room to hear the tail end of Irv reporting what had happened.

"So, these are reinforcements?" Tik asked. "What about Prosperity? This isn't enough to defend us."

Lena couldn't argue with his assessment. "Yes, this is it for now. I know it's not enough; we'll just have to start training as soon as the sun is up. We brought more weapons, but we can't keep trying for information, or help. It won't be that long before we know exactly who the Fort is going against, because they'll be fighting for their survival, or we'll be facing them along with Cole's men."

Mellow stood up and started clearing plates, nodding at the sandwich and apple in front of the empty chair. "Eat, Lena. We've all learned to be pragmatic; no one's going to moan about what we don't have."

Lena didn't know what she expected the conversation to accomplish. The people with information were exhausted, and the people who'd stayed at the farm didn't know what to ask. She bit into the sandwich and tasted bacon and butter. It was the best thing she could ever remember eating.

"We'll talk again over breakfast," she said after swallowing her bite. "Do we have beds for everyone?"

Before Ava could get the word out in answer, the sound of a horse galloping into the yard tore everyone's attention away.

"Stay here," Scott said, reaching for his rifle. "Tik, grab your weapon and come with me."

No one else left the room, but everyone drew weapons, some from holsters, and others from where they'd left them resting against the wall. Lena motioned for people to be quiet, so that she could hear what was going on.

"Deb," Scott called. "Bring the medical kit."

Lena ran to the hall. The young girl who must be Mahir's sister sat on the bottom of the stairs, head in hands. Evan leaned on the wall. They were both exhausted.

"Pallavi!" Mahir came running from the dining room and squeezed himself beside his sister, wrapping his arms around her.

"It's us," Evan said. "They're coming for us first. Four days."

"Marley, get your ass over to Redstone," Irv said. "One of you guys from Crystal needs to go back and get more fighters."

CHAPTER THIRTY-FIVE

For the next few minutes, everyone was in motion. Scott said that he would provide fresh horses for the people looking for reinforcements.

Deb had hustled Pallavi and Mahir into the parlor. While Maya and Jason dragged mattresses and blankets in, Deb tended to Pallavi. Lena stood at the door watching. It wouldn't be comfortable, and everyone else would be sleeping on their box spring, but it would do as a temporary barracks. She glanced around and saw Evan leaning against the wall beside the door, his eyes closed.

"Evan?" She had to call his name twice more before he opened his eyes. "Let Deb look at your hand. Do you have any other injuries?"

"I don't think so. At least nothing hurts." He lifted his hand and nodded to the wound on the bicep. "I think this is almost healed."

"Well, let her look at you anyway," she said. "We need everybody as fit as possible."

He followed her into the room and sat on the couch beside Pallavi. The confidence that he carried like a second skin was gone. Something happened to them. She wouldn't ask now, but soon. They had to know exactly what had happened.

Deb finished with Pallavi and turned her attentions to Evan, moving him to a chair away from the children. Whether she'd done it on purpose or not, Lena was happy for the small sense of privacy while she talked to them.

"I'm glad we found you, Pallavi." She didn't want the girl going to sleep and then suddenly waking up wondering what was going to become of her. "Did your brother tell you what happened?"

"Yes," Pallavi answered, her voice barely audible. "Thank you for taking my brother in. We won't bother you. As soon as it's safe, we'll head out."

"I'm sorry you lost your dad."

"They went and got him," Mahir said to Pallavi. "He's buried right here. Near some other people."

That small gravesite was going to be much bigger, Lena realized. Win or lose, there would be death. "I understand you might want to leave," Lena said. "It's going to be dangerous around here. But if you want to stay, you're welcome."

Pallavi's head jerked up to meet Lena's gaze. "Why would you take us in?"

"It's gonna be pretty dangerous everywhere; you need a home. There's room here. Well, there will be."

Mahir was grinning, it was nice to see it. Pallavi still didn't look convinced.

"Look, I get it," Lena said. "There's a chance that we'll lose the fight. But if it looks like that, we'll run. He can have the farm, but he can't have us. They'll take us in at Redstone, or Crystal. And I'm pretty sure Prosperity will be happy to see us if it comes to that."

"Can you guarantee that Cole won't get me?" Pallavi asked. "If I stay here, can you promise that?"

Her words made Lena more determined than ever to find out what had happened to Pallavi and Evan, but now it was time for the truth. "I can promise that we'll do everything to make sure it won't happen. At least here, you're not the only pretty, young girl. And I'm sure Mellow can show you how to defend yourself. I can also promise no matter what, I'll do whatever it takes to stop Cole from getting at you, or anyone else on this farm."

Pallavi looked at Mahir, and then around the room. "Yes, I think we would like to stay."

The whiskey wasn't helping. Evan felt like his whole body was shaking with fatigue. He couldn't leave the room because he wouldn't sleep for wondering what he was missing.

The room was full, only the children upstairs, and Pallavi. She'd fallen asleep at the table, so Keith carried her to sleep in the kid's room.

An hour after the two riders had gone for reinforcements, three men and two women came up the front steps, rifles in one hand and bags of ammunition in the other. Their skin was dark, but that could have been the sun. High cheekbones and strong bodies, they looked similar enough to be family. He guessed they were smallholders wanting in the fight. Evan had no idea who'd passed on the information, but five more guns wouldn't hurt.

"You don't have to put us up," the older woman, Alsoomse, said. "We're only a short ride away. You got an alarm?"

"We have some flares," Keith said. "We can send them up at the first sign of trouble. What about you? If they come your way?"

"We'll take a few of them flares, if you don't mind," she answered for the group. "That Cole might pass us by, but if he don't, he'll not hit us until you're down. We're too small to worry about. Might cost him a man or two just to take us."

Are the smallholders organized? Evan thought they were individuals, but this woman sounded like she was representing more than the people who came with her. "What makes you think that?" he asked.

"They took some of our boys," she said. "Just like always, our kids don't matter to you white folks. Some of the Cree said the plagues were payback. But nothing really changes."

"Then why are you helping?" Lena asked.

"Well, there's white folk and there's white folk. You seem to be willing to mind your own business. We like that in a neighbor."

Lena chuckled. "Us too."

"Why do you think they're coming here first?" The woman asked. "I mean, you heard it, yes, but why here? Seems like they'd be better off with a town. Take one of them down, and no one will be able to stand."

Everyone looked to Evan. "We only heard the facts, but I'm guessing one of two reasons, maybe both. They need food. The fort doesn't grow anything. They have stocks, but they must be running out. The farm has food, and lots of it. The other reason is the location. Setting up here means they are closer to Crystal, and no farther away from Redstone than before. It can't be easy living up there in the winter, either."

The woman spoke to her companions in a language Evan didn't recognize. Then she turned back to the group. "It's late. We need six flares. We'll be only twenty minutes away. We'll come in shooting, so be ready." She looked around the table. "And get some sleep."

Keith led them to the basement where the ammunition and emergency supplies were stored. When they came back, the visitors had new bags in hand. The ammunition traded for flares and other items.

CHAPTER THIRTY-SIX

This was possibly the longest day of Lena's life. Before she hit her bed, she still needed to get a plan in order. In a couple of hours, it would be daylight. How soon could they start training for the attack?

"We need to split people up, so we can attack on all flanks," Tik said, breaking into her thoughts.

She looked around before answering. Everyone looked like they were about to fall asleep where they sat. "We don't need everyone for this. You should all get some rest; it will be an early morning."

Keith gave Deb a kiss on the cheek. "Lena's right. No need for everyone to be worn out tomorrow. Lena, Tik, and I can figure out the next steps."

"What about me?" Scott asked. "And Evan. We've got some knowledge."

Lena closed her eyes and let them figure out who would stay. She didn't have the energy.

"Yeah, lots of us have knowledge," Keith answered. "But we need some of those people for tomorrow. You, Evan, Irv, and the people from Crystal need to do some training while the three of

us sleep. I'll leave notes for you. We can all talk tomorrow afternoon and rejig the plan as needed."

Lena opened her eyes and watched everyone drift off to their
beds. "We can't take too long."

"It'll go fast now we're alone," Tik said. "Fewer sides to any
disagreement."

Decisions usually took twice as long as necessary while
everyone had their turn to talk. If it wasn't so life and death, it
would be funny. She trusted that Tik's gang experience would
help. Keith's background was murky, but he knew how to handle a
fight. Lena didn't know why they needed her.

"How many do we have? And what skills?" Keith asked. "If we
get that down, and an idea of our strategy, we can be done in no
time."

Lena pulled a sheet of paper from the pile on the table and
grabbed a pencil. "There's us, original farm. That's seven adults
and two kids. Everyone can shoot a rifle and draw a bow. I've
killed a man," she looked at Keith and Tik. They both nodded.
"So, three of us know we can do it, the others only in theory, but
I'm feeling confident about it. There's Pallavi and Mahir, we don't
know their skills, so let's say they don't have any for the purpose
of planning. We have six fighters from Crystal."

"Seventeen isn't too bad," Tik said. "We can split people into
three groups: face on, left flank, right flank."

"Will Deb fight?" Lena asked. "Will we need her more as a
medic?"

"If it goes the way I think," Tik said. "It will be too fast for
us to deal with wounds until after. I'm more worried about coor-
dinating the attacks. And how we'll integrate anyone who
joins us."

"Our Cree friends?" Lena asked.

"Them, and maybe some reinforcements from our new allies."
Keith took the paper and stared at the names. "The Cree know
who we are. I'm guessing they have their own plan. We don't want

anyone else jumping in and confusing the good guys and bad guys."

"Will they just do that?" Lena asked, thinking she should have held back the messengers until they had a plan.

"No. They're trained," Tik said. "I've talked to the people from Crystal. If this was a gang war, reinforcements — or rather, people switching sides — would check with the leader before joining a fight."

It was getting harder to keep from laying her head on the table. Lena pinched her leg to stave off sleep for another few minutes. "I think that means someone should be here, directing traffic so to speak. Before you say anything, that's not me. I'm going to be fighting."

She saw that Keith and Tik wanted to argue. But they must have seen something other than exhaustion on her face.

Keith pulled a new sheet of paper off the pile. "Fine, we'll know tomorrow who's got the least chance of surviving a gunfight. Maybe Mahir. I'm not sure he's got the strength to stand up to a rifle recoil anyway. And he seems like a smart kid. Knew to come to us when his dad passed. He's just going to be directing traffic anyway."

Keith divided the paper into three sections and started writing names.

It was amazing what a solid night's sleep could do. Evan's wounds only itched now, the pain gone, and so too were the bandages. He stood beside Lena and watched their little army prove their skills.

"It's hard to say if they are ready," he said. "Not using ammo is leaving out a lot of opportunities."

"Can we spare any?" Lena asked.

She knew the answer, so Evan didn't bother to speak.

The fighters were doing a fair job of running in a coordinated attack, and, as Keith and Tik said, it's more about getting them to work as a team than improve their shooting. "The kids are doing better than the adults in some places," he said. "Even Mahir has found his skill."

"He's still staying here to coordinate, not fight," Lena said. "I haven't changed my mind. And he might need to defend himself. He's fast with the knife if he can get in close."

Evan nodded. "We can spare a few rounds for Pallavi and Mahir to learn how to fire a weapon. The terrain is going to be our biggest asset. If we can keep them in the woods, it will even the odds." The farm was positioned ideally for defense. It might be downhill, but the hills were covered in a thick band of trees, riddled with streams and caves. There was only one way through, and it wouldn't take more than two or three abreast.

"After lunch," Lena said. "I don't want them hitting one of our precious few soldiers."

The close in skirmishes were working fine against their opponents. The only problem Evan could see was that real enemies would be desperate for the kill. And now, when fear wasn't driving him, and he had time to think through everything, he knew there weren't enough people.

"Lena, we need to change up everything. Can we call in Keith and Tik?"

"It's not going to work, is it?" she asked. Then whistled and waved her arm to get Tik and Keith's attention. "It can't hurt to let the others think they are getting better until we come up with another plan."

"The real fighters already know," Evan said.

In the kitchen, Mellow and Scott were preparing lunch. The teapot was on and there was room to sit and talk. Evan wanted their input. He hoped they would have a novel approach since neither were really fighters.

When the two men joined Evan and Lena, he laid out his idea. "Normal combat won't work. If we were all soldiers, maybe it would be enough, but we're farmers and kids mostly."

"Don't underestimate the power of defending your home," Tik said. "But, yeah. If this turf war was going on in my old gang, we wouldn't fight like an army."

"Guerrilla warfare," Scott said. "Harry them until they weaken?"

Evan hadn't expected to be upstaged. "Yeah. Like a pack of wolves, well, sort of. We pick at them, wound them, kill if we can, but it's a hit and run strategy."

"Do we have time to get ready for that?" Lena asked. "And what about reinforcements?"

"We have all the skills," Tik said. "I don't know why we didn't think about it last night. Maybe after lunch we'll take them all into the woods and challenge them to capture one of us. That should tell us if they can do it."

"Mahir will need to be told what to do if reinforcements arrive," Evan said. "If we do this, we won't be easy to find. But we still won't be confused with the enemy. Guerrilla fighting is too subtle for Cole."

Mellow started piling food on the table; sandwiches, fruit, cheese, everything portable. "They should drink water before you start. We don't have enough travel cups for everyone. I think that should be on the next foraging trip, things to carry food."

Lena went to the door and blew the whistle that signaled lunch. "Get ready to explain, guys. We need them out and training as soon as possible."

Evan stood. "Scott can tell them. Keith, Tik, and I need to put our heads together to make this a real challenge."

CHAPTER THIRTY-SEVEN

Pallavi made sure she stepped in Tik's footprints. Not that he left many, the man walked like he was a ghost. In all her time running between the farm and shelter, she'd never thought to learn how to sneak through the trees this well.

Two days of playing war ended this morning when Cole's men were first sighted crossing the rise in the distance. Now, here she was with Tik and Mahir, checking on the traps they'd set to stall the first attack.

Her brother was out here because one of the Crystal fighters had fallen and twisted her ankle. Now Enid was in the relative safety of the farmhouse, and Mahir was with her.

Tik directed them to the first trap. The fallen branches and leaves they'd used to obscure the pit were blown aside, revealing the hole meant to stop a horse and maybe injure the rider. She hated that the animals would suffer, but horses were an advantage, and Cole's army had too many of those.

She joined Mahir in rearranging the cover, wanting to talk, but knowing it was dangerous.

When the hole was covered again, Tik beckoned them toward him. Leaning in close so he could keep his voice just audible, he said, "The storm probably did the same to all of them, if we split up, we can fix it faster. Do you know where the other four are?"

Pallavi nodded and saw Mahir grin as he did the same. Was her brother enjoying this too much? Or did he think it was just a game? Either answer made her cold with fear.

"You and Mahir go to the traps downhill, by the stream and that trail. I'll take the others. Be careful and get back here. I think we can arrange a few more surprises."

They parted ways. Pallavi tried to imitate Tik's movements, but without him there to lead, she sounded like an elephant trampling trees. *I hope that's just fear amplifying the noise.*

The trap by the trail was still in place, so they moved on. The one by the stream had dislodged. It was a stack of rocks that were set to fall when someone knocked a branch. The branch was so much in the way of anyone passing that it was guaranteed to trigger the fall. Overnight, something had tripped it.

Pallavi helped Mahir pile the rocks again and replace the branch. There was no body or signs of wounds under the rocks. She hoped whatever triggered the trap had been faster than a human.

"Well, what's this?" the voice cut through the quiet around her. Pallavi dropped the stone she was carrying and looked up. A man, short and dirty, stood grinning at her like she was lunch. Mahir was nowhere in sight. She hoped he had the sense to stay hidden.

"I asked you a question, girl." The man took a step toward her.

"Nothing. I'm just trying to trap a deer. We need meat." Pallavi slid her hands into her pocket. She'd taken a throwing knife as her weapon. It was in a sheath in the right pocket of her pants.

"That's going to pulverize it, if the deer don't just skip away," the man said, taking another step forward. "I can show you how, if you can do me a favor." He undid the buckle on his belt.

"I don't need your help," Pallavi said. She grasped the haft of the knife, fingers damp with sweat and gritty with dirt.

"Then I'll just take the favor," he said, scrabbling up the small slope.

When he was in arm's reach, Pallavi slid the knife out of the sheath and threw.

It stuck in his throat. He took two more steps and then collapsed.

Pallavi ran to a bush and threw up her lunch.

"You killed him," Mahir said, standing over the body.

Pallavi was still shaking from the ordeal. If she hadn't watched Evan kill at the fort, she might not have acted. But what he'd done woke her to the brutality of her new world. Now Mahir faced it.

She hoped they had enough time. The man wasn't quiet, so maybe he was alone, scouting the area. "Yes, that's what is going to happen, Mahir. I'm sorry, but you might have to kill someone too. You have to remember how evil these people are."

He looked from her to the body and back. "We should go. This isn't our fight, we can get away from the Fort. We can find another place to live." He reached to tug her away from the trap and the body.

"Keep your voice down, Mahir." Pallavi scrambled past her brother, looking for a hiding place for the body. "I'm not leaving. Remember what happened last time I tried to go west?"

"But now they will be here, fighting,' he said, following her. "They won't be out kidnapping girls."

Pallavi stopped searching and turned to Mahir, taking his shoulders in her hands, trying to get him to understand. "These aren't the only bad people out here," she said, calmly. "There will always be someone willing to take what they want and hurt anyone who gets in their way."

He blinked at tears. "Dad was right. It is too dangerous."

Pallavi bit her lip to silence the sob of grief. When she was sure her voice would be steady, she said, "Yes, but he was wrong to lock us away. There are also good people. The people fighting with us are good people. We will find a home with them. Being alone is the danger, Mahir. Please stop trying to run away from this and help me hide the body."

She could feel his body trembling under her hands. Pallavi pulled Mahir into a hug. "It will get better. You will have friends, we will—"

"Get killed if you keep talking," Tik said. He took in the scene with one look and pulled the shovel from his supplies. "Dig a shallow grave. It will keep the carrion birds away a bit longer. I've found a place we can set another trap. Then we go back. You can tell us what happened when we're home. No one talks until I say so."

Evan had been checking traps for an hour. Time to report back, not that he had much to report. There was no sign of anything out of place. He was tempted to ride toward the enemy to assess what was coming but knew that it could put him in danger and leave the farm without a fighter.

Over the last two days, they'd managed to dig six pits on the most obvious approaches, and ten or more other traps to delay, damage, or kill anyone who tripped them. No one good would be passing this way, and they would be easy to disarm when the fight was over.

He grabbed a branch and wiped out his footprints, ready to get back to the horse and return to make his report.

"I know what we were told." A woman's voice.

Evan placed the branch on the ground and moved in a crouch to the closest cover. They were west of him.

"Cole won't be happy." Another woman.

The sound of crushed leaves and twigs rubbing on fabric preceded the appearance of three of Cole's fighters: two women and a man, all well-fed and unwashed. Evan lifted his rifle.

"Cole ain't never happy since that girl escaped," the man said. "Didn't seem to care about Davey getting hisself killed, just that bit of sweetness for his bed."

They were only two steps from his trap. All three walking together, not seeming alert to any danger, not even the normal ones on a hillside. Evan willed them to fall into the pit. They came to a stop. The man drank from a flask, the older woman lit a joint and passed it along.

She coughed out the smoke. "He'll be happy if we get one of them farmers. Maybe another clean young thing."

Evan scanned the area, looking for something to get them moving again. There were no convenient stones to throw, nothing to startle them. The pit was between his hiding place and the three soldiers. He couldn't let them pass. If the farm lost the element of surprise, they wouldn't stand a chance.

He reached down and found a broken twig, snapping it to get their attention. They turned toward the sound as if their heads were connected on a string.

"Just an animal," the younger woman said, stubbing the joint out on the sole of her boot. "Liam, go check it out."

The man looked like he was going to argue, then he shrugged and started toward Evan.

No one had their weapons ready; sloppy.

Evan needed them all to come. He stepped out from behind his cover and raised his hands, holding his rifle in this right. Shooting them would make too much noise, but he wasn't going to let them take it.

The older woman raised her gun, a pistol. She was no fighter; the gun was pretty, but Evan could see how old and badly maintained it was.

"Don't shoot," he said, trying to make his voice quaver with fear.

The man was only one step away from falling into the pit, the two women stupidly moved to stand beside him.

"You from the Fort?" he asked, trying to keep them from shooting.

"What's it to you?" The younger woman raised her own gun, a rifle, well-maintained.

"I got something Cole needs," he said, lowering his hands. "Information on the farm." He reached into his pocket. "It's good, who wants to take it? I'll go back with you. I want to join up."

They exchanged a glance and Evan bit his cheek to stop the smile. All three stepped forward. A crack and then a cloud of dust as they dropped through.

Bringing his rifle to his shoulder, ready to fire if it was needed, Evan walked over to look into the pit. It was deep. When they dug it, they broke through the roof of a cave formed by the roots of the trees, and some boulders. They'd dropped rocks in the bottom and covered the top.

The sun shone through another break. Evan could see the man was dead, his head facing up, his body facing down. The older woman had fallen on the man's rifle and the barrel stuck up through her chest. The younger woman was coughing, blood gurgling each time she breathed. As he watched, the light went out and the noise stopped.

CHAPTER THIRTY-EIGHT

Lena surveyed the farm from the back porch. Almost everyone was back, and it was time to get her update; any changes to the plans needed to be discussed now. In a couple of hours, she'd be hiding behind something and waiting for battle. Right now, she needed to soak in the peace. A thought floated through her mind as she tried to empty her tension in meditation: this was inevitable. If she was still in New Surrey, she'd be fighting a gang, or some other force determined to take what they wanted. Or, maybe, just fighting with Brian. At least here, on the farm, there was a chance to survive to a life she wanted, not just waiting for the next rule to take away the remnants of her freedom, or the next bully to take her life.

The farm lay in a valley between hills, none of them high, but enough that it felt sheltered. The hills were forested, and no one at the farm had thought to clear them to make more arable land. *Next year. And maybe a guest house past the barn, and maybe a few rows of hops to make beer.*

Three riders cleared the trees. Lena couldn't make out the faces, but she knew they were the last of her fighters. Something about their movements on horseback made them seem friendly.

It only took minutes as they wove through the final line of traps and raced to the house.

"Sorry, we're late," Jose, one of the Crystal fighters, said. "A few scouts are already close. They won't be reporting back."

It was said so matter-of-factly. Did the woman have no emotional reaction? Is this what she would be like? Her friends? Lena left the questions unspoken and led the three into the dining room-cum-headquarters.

The reports took no time at all. Three groups had encountered scouts. Pallavi told the facts of her encounter. Lena could tell by the way Mahir stared at his sister that there was more to it, but it would wait until the battle was over.

"Okay, no changes to the plan, then?" Lena asked. No one offered any comment. She couldn't let them leave without saying something inspiring. It was hard to find words for the group of strangers and family gathered. "I'm not great at pep talks," she said. Then, clearing her throat, she added, "This is going to be chaos. We might not see each other until this is over, one way or another. Fight hard. Be safe. Come home."

She hugged Scott, wishing he was fighting beside her, but knowing the strategy behind the teams made more sense than her wishes. Mellow and Tik left to say their own goodbyes. Deb and Keith were whispering in the corner.

"It's hard," Ava said, moving close. "But they are as ready as you can make them. You have to concentrate on your own fight now."

"Is that how you are handling sending Maya and Jason into the fight?" Lena played with a knife on the table, trying to get her mind off what was coming.

"No," Ava said. "They are with two of the best fighters we have. I'm worried sick about them. I just figure when the fighting starts, I'll be busy staying alive and the kids will be fine."

"Liar," Lena said. She put the knife down.

"Yeah," Ava said. "I just know that if I try to do anything other than fight with my team, the kids will be in more danger."

Lena hugged Ava. "We'll all survive."

"I'll hold you to that," Ava said.

It was time. Lena called for attention. "Get your stocks and we'll go."

She turned to the woman who was stuck at the farmhouse. "You have the map with the location of all traps?"

"I made a bunch of copies," she said. "I'll hand them out to any reinforcements."

Lena glanced at them. "Good work, Enid." Lena could feel the loose threads of the plan trying to unravel. Logically there was no way to control every last detail, or, if she was honest, none of the details. The one that tugged most at her confidence was her neighbors. "If any of the Cree fighters come by, make sure they know the plan and give them what they need."

Enid shifted her weight in the chair. "I will. Lena, you don't need to worry about anything now. You just go out and do your part, keep your team alive and kill as many of Cole's men as you can."

"Easier said than done," Lena said. "I trust you, I'm just new to this."

"That's why you're with me," Evan said, striding into the room and holding out her weapons.

Evan blinked away sweat. He could hear the thump of footsteps and the occasional word called out. The wait had been quiet, no sounds of distant shots, no screams. This might be the first encounter. He looked to where the others were hidden. Lena crouched in the shadow of a boulder, Rick lying behind a fallen tree, Mary overhead on a branch of another tree, Louise shrunk in the shadows, her face covered in mud. He nodded to them to be alert and wait for the right moment. They knew to let Cole's soldiers walk into the open, unaware there was an attack waiting. Their entire first assault was planned to exploit the assumption that there would be no resistance — that no one knew Cole was coming.

Whoever shot the first bullet would end that advantage.

Two men broke through to the clearing, one reached back to wave others in.

Evan slowed his breath and sharpened his focus. He raised his weapon and sighted on one target.

"Five minutes," the lead man said. "Just five minutes rest."

There were ten men in the clearing, and they arranged themselves stupidly, all clustered in the center of the space. No one would be caught in the crossfire, none of Evan's team would get hurt.

He trusted that everyone had picked a target and would be ready to take their second shot at a different target.

The men were still milling about, arguing over whether to stay, or go on and be the ones to take the farm.

Evan's shot would signal the rest of the team to fire. He put his finger on the trigger and waited for them to settle for this rest.

"Fine," the first man said, loudly enough to override the chatter. "We'll go in a minute. I need a drink." He reached for a flask, one that probably didn't contain water.

Evan took in a breath and held it, ready to squeeze the trigger.

A scream tore through the quiet. The men in the clearing scattered. Evan's shot went wide, missing his target, but killing another. His team fired, but only two others went down. The rest were scattering, some back the way they came, some toward the farm, and some simply into the trees.

One of their traps had kicked off the attack.

As the clearing emptied of Cole's men, Evan's rushed to fill it, weapons held ready.

"You go after them," he said, pointing Mary and Rick to the men running to the farm."

"I can go up the trail," Lena said. "You catch up when you've found the rest." She didn't wait for him to agree.

"So much for my leadership," Evan said. Then, turning to Louise, he said, "I counted three running blindly."

"Yeah, two east, one south," she pointed as she spoke. "I'll go south, do you want me to double back to you or to Lena when I'm done?"

"Lena," he said. "With any luck, we'll catch her before she does anything else stupid." He wanted to go after Lena now, but having three enemy soldiers running free was too risky.

Two hours later, Evan pulled his new team into a huddle. Lena was still missing, but he couldn't worry about that, he had four new people to worry about. Mahir and Pallavi were inseparable and now his team. The neighbors had joined the fight; Keme, one of the sons, was keeping lookout a few feet away in the bushes. And Irv, wounded but refusing to leave the fight.

No longer silent, the battles around them snapped with gunfire and screams. Men trapped in pits, crushed under falling stones shot and left to die.

A group of Cole's men were reforming a unit yards away. If Evan could get his team near, killing them would be easy, and he wouldn't hesitate this time. "You take anyone in the back of the group," he said to Keme. "Stay uphill so there's no danger of friendly fire."

"I'm not stupid," Keme said. "Been hunting these hills since I was a kid. You make sure you don't fuck up and I'll do my job. Can you scream like an eagle?"

"No," Evan said.

Keme laughed. "Me neither. Just shout and I'll start shooting." He crept away from the group, disappearing into the shadows and undergrowth.

"Better that you reminded him," Irv said. "No place for assumptions."

Evan drew Mahir and Pallavi to him. "I want you to shoot from this side. Just keep hammering at the middle of the group."

Pallavi nodded.

"Irv, we'll head a bit downhill, pick off any runners."

"Because I'm hurt?" Irv looked pissed off.

"No, because you're a better shot than these two combined," he said.

He waited until Mahir and Pallavi were in place before following Irv to a blind downhill from the group.

"Now!"

Bullets answered him.

At first the enemy was shocked into standing there. Then, after a few of them fell dead, they started shooting back. It wasn't effective. They only had a hint of where the shots were coming from. Keme kept moving, staying in his zone, but shooting from slightly different locations.

The fire from Pallavi and Mahir was constant; no moments for anyone to come out of the cover they'd found and fire back.

Two men managed to slip away. Irv killed the first, then Evan shot the other. A few more rounds of ammunition sounded, and then silence. They were gone. Evan stood and waved his team back to the rendezvous. He turned to tell Irv to lead the way.

Irv sat with his hand on his belly, pushing the rifle toward Evan.

He coughed and groaned. "Take the gun," he managed to squeeze out.

Evan tried to lift Irv's hand and see how bad it was.

"No, boy. You go back. I'm done," Irv's words were strangled. "I got a knife," he added. "Just go."

CHAPTER THIRTY-NINE

Running through the trees, Lena listened for her companions. The original teams had dissolved over time as they lost fighters. She shied away from thinking about how small her force was now. As far as she could tell, about a third were dead and the army from the Fort kept coming. She'd caught a glimpse of Maya a few minutes ago, running ahead of two of the men from the Fort, leading them to a trap, not racing away in fear.

Now she was acting as bait for a group of Cole's men, too. The trap was only a few yards ahead and it was tempting to speed up, but critical that she keep just in their sight. They were stupid. There were ten or more of them, and as far as they knew she was only one. They should break off, leaving one of them to chase her. But they were caught up in the excitement of the chase and she wasn't going to waste the opportunity.

Six of her fighters were waiting at the trap, ready to finish off any who escaped.

Lena saw the marker, a tiny cairn, and swung right, running into the stream and turning to follow the flow, holding onto the illusion until she heard the screams.

There was no pleasure in the sound for Lena. These men

might be the enemy, but they were humans; only a few wrong decisions put them in opposition to her.

She waded out of the stream and bent to catch her breath.

"Good job," a whisper came from the shadows.

Lena slid her hands toward the sheath of her knife.

"Don't," the voice whispered again. "I'm a friend, but I won't hesitate to defend myself." The speaker stepped into the dim light. Her neighbor.

"Alsoomse, are you alone?" Lena asked.

She nodded. "Easier to creep up and do some damage. I don't want to join with your group if that's why you're asking."

Lena looked behind her; the screams were shriller, but fewer of them. "Do you know how it's going?"

"'Bout what you expect. It will turn soon, but I can't tell who'll come out on top." She stepped closer. "You can't keep the battle in the trees. Even these idiots will learn to pull you out in the open. That happens, you better be ready to see death on a grand scale. Horses, men, women, yours, his — it will be fast and ugly. No time for catching your breath, no time to worry about anything but the next bullet."

Lena looked closer at her neighbor. "How do you know?"

She grinned, but there was humor in it. "First coupla years, we had to work hard to keep what's ours. This Cole guy? He ain't the first, he won't be the last."

"Thanks," Lena said. "Maybe we should take the initiative, draw a few out in the open?"

"You do that, you better slaughter them, make it a lesson."

Evan's wounds screamed pain at him. His old ones and the scrapes and bruises he'd accumulated today were like a harmony of agony. This time it helped him focus. The only one he worried about was the near miss of a bullet. It had grazed his right bicep and at some point it would seize the muscle, and that was his trigger hand.

All the traps in his area were sprung; only a few of the enemy had survived, maybe that was good. They'd report back their losses, maybe the enemy would retreat. Maybe, but not likely.

His still had three people with him. Keme and a couple of people from Crystal. The band of trees was thinning at this elevation. Evan and his team hid in the best cover they could find, looking out over the open hill.

"If we go out, we need horses," Keme said. "I can go round up some from the last trap."

Cole's men had mostly been on foot, a good strategy for fighting in the trees and undergrowth where there were too many places for a horse to break a leg. The last group must have come into the woods, hoping to see a way through. The only obvious path from here to the farm was a narrow trail through the trees. More like a funnel than a good attack approach.

"The horses aren't going anywhere," Evan said. "If we come out in the open, I need a good reason."

The field in front of them was scrubby grass and rocks. None of the rocks big enough to hide behind. Evan knew from his visits to the fort that a horse could pick his way through, but not gallop without risking an injury.

The best use of this stretch of land was to bring Cole's forces together for the assault on the farm. It would cost Cole a lot of men, but he had enough and didn't seem to care about sacrificing them.

As he watched, three men rode into sight. Cole, and two well-armed soldiers.

Evan moved back a few feet. "Get the horses," he said to Keme. "I'm going after Cole. The rest of you find another team."

Keme ran toward the last battle without argument.

"It's stupid to go alone," the man from Crystal said. "Three of them. Only takes one bullet to stop you."

Evan listened for Keme. "I'll use the horses for cover. He won't know I'm coming until I'm within range."

"Nice plan." He shook his head. "You've noticed how well the plan is going, right?"

Keme led four horses toward them.

"This might be the only opportunity we have." Evan took the reins.

"We'll pass the word. If Cole's here, he's changing tactics. You kill him, or he kills you, we need to be ready." Keme pointed to the smallest horse. "They'll follow her. You run beside her as long as you can."

Evan said goodbye and led the horses to the edge of the tree line. Cole was waiting for something and it wouldn't be anything good.

Lena knew her neighbor was right, but it was hard to make the decision to leave cover. The traps were working well; they should have made more of them. Surely by now, most of them were sprung.

"I need to see what's going on," she said to her team. "You keep doing the same thing, but find others, get news, and be prepared to draw back."

"Them reinforcements would be welcome," Louise said.

"We can't count on them," Lena said, hating that it was true. "We need to bring this fight in. Try to trap them on the path and we can pick them off."

"Hope Cole runs out of fighters before we do," Louise said. "Don't do anything stupid, Lena."

"It's only stupid if I fail," Lena said.

As her team drifted deeper into the woods, Lena moved north. She'd come out of the woods just at the side of the path leading to the farm. If anything was happening, she'd still be able to run.

A few feet of open space separated Lena from the vantage point the last tree would give. She could hear voices ahead; not a crowd, but a conversation. She couldn't risk stepping out without knowing where they were, and who. She lay on the ground and crawled forward, hoping the men wouldn't think to look down.

They were close. Close enough that she could have put a bullet in one before they turned. Unfortunately, it was also close enough that the two remaining men would have time to retaliate.

They were on horseback, facing away from her. Even so, she couldn't run for the tree without drawing attention. Lena held her breath and listened.

"Don't like it, Cole," a man in a blue shirt said. He kept talking, but Lena couldn't hear.

Newton Cole was right there, ready to be killed.

Her rifle was behind her. Now she understood how decisions could be stupid. Leaving it there made it easier to crawl forward. But now, she had to crawl back, risking noise and attention.

She had a knife, but it wasn't a throwing one and the men were too far away for her to run in and stab.

As she struggled to find a plan, Lena heard the approach of horses. The men turned, and she followed their gaze.

"Grab them," Cole said.

Lena pushed herself to her feet. What Cole couldn't see from their angle was Evan running beside the lead horse, rifle in hand.

Evan raised his rifle, all he had to do was take out Cole. The other two could wait, and if he didn't survive, well, it was worth it.

The horses ran past him as he stood to take aim. He touched the trigger and squeezed.

A scream from the woods at the side surprised him and knocked his aim off. Then the screamer barreled from out of the trees toward the men. Lena. She had her own rifle, but threw stones as she ran, hitting the horses and scattering them. Separating Cole from his men and creating chaos for them.

From outside, it was like a target, Cole spinning on his horse, trying to get control while reaching for his weapon. He pulled a pistol, wrong choice.

Evan aimed again, but one of the other men took the bullet because his horse ran him to the center of the mob.

He aimed again. This time winging Cole. Now Lena was in the middle of the mess. She grabbed Cole's last man and yanked.

Cole aimed and shot, the bullet not even coming close to Lena, landing in the horse's flank. It bucked, the man fell, Lena stabbed him through the throat to his brain.

That left Cole.

The milling horses were still in panic, but now they were lining up to run. Cole fought to stop his from joining.

Evan had one more shot; Lena ran for Cole.

"Down!" Evan aimed as Lena dropped to the ground.

Everything went silent as he placed his finger on the trigger. Then he heard his heartbeat, then he squeezed.

Evan felt the kick in his shoulder and sensations came flooding back. Noise, heat, grit, pain. Cole jerked in the saddle, looked at his chest, and collapsed.

CHAPTER FORTY

Lena felt the ground thud with the horses' stomping. She heard the shot but couldn't do anything but roll to avoid being trampled. Then the horses moved away. She rolled over to face Newton Cole's body.

She jerked away and scrambled to her feet. Evan was standing on the other side of Cole, holding the reins of a horse who really didn't want to be there.

"We can't just carry him back," he said. "And we need to prove he's dead."

Lena wiped her hair back from her face. It was going to be hard to put Cole on the back of the horse. "Can you lift him?"

Evan tried to raise his arm and winced. "I was thinking more of making a frame and dragging him in."

Lena pointed back to her hiding place. "There are lots of downed branches back there. Cut all the straps you can from the tack and we'll use that to tie him."

An hour later, Evan and Lena emerged from the path to see

groups of people fighting on the edge of the farmland. Apparently, the narrow path hadn't been as much help as expected.

"You wouldn't happen to have a flare with you?" Lena asked, regretting the loss of her pack at the first battle.

"Nope, but look what I found when I went through the saddlebags." He held up an air horn.

"You could have told me," Lena said holding out her hand for the horn.

"More fun to reveal it now." He placed the horn in her hand. "We should probably move forward so they can see it's us."

Lena tugged on the reins and stepped into clear view. She activated the horn and kept sounding it until the fighting stopped. She smiled at the speed that Cole's men reacted. They thought they had won.

She took a few steps forward. Her voice wouldn't carry far, but people would pass on her words. "I need someone with some authority."

"Cole is on his way, lady," one of the attackers said. He crudely grabbed his crotch and made thrusting motions.

"No, he isn't," she said.

Evan dragged the frame to the side and tipped the body onto the ground.

"You have two choices," Lena said. "Give up, we'll deal with you fairly. Or just go. If you don't come back, we won't come for you."

The man who'd spoken stepped forward. "Fuck, it is Cole." He looked at Lena. "You did this?"

Lena shook her head. "We did it. We'll keep doing it if you don't leave us alone. This could be you next time."

"You're just a bunch of farmers," the man said. "You got lucky."

Lena shook her head. "Not lucky. And, if you don't go now, and stay away, I promise you it will be painful, and we won't stop until you are all gone."

"Okay, we're done for now," the man said. "Cole underestimated you. The next one might not."

Lena grinned. "I think Cole overestimated you. One more thing. You'll free all those boys you took. If they want to go back to their families, you'll not only let them go, you'll give them supplies and you'll make sure they get there safely."

"How will you know what we did?"

"Don't take any chances," Lena said. "Any more stupid questions?"

The man didn't answer. He pulled a flag out of his pocket. It was a skull and crossbones. They thought they were pirates.

When he waved the flag, all the men from the Fort ran. Within moments the only people in sight were Lena's allies. A wave of exhaustion overwhelmed her. Her legs gave out, and the world went dark.

"How bad?" Lena asked as soon as she woke.

"Five dead, seven badly injured, and most of us with some kind of cut, bruise, or sprain. There won't be much work on the farm for the next couple of days."

She remembered thinking it was worse than that. "And you?" Lena nodded at Ava's bandaged arm.

"I fell. It's not bad. We have to get these people fed and settled." Ava helped Lena stand. "Although some of them are already in bed."

"The reinforcements?"

"I sent runners to turn them back. Well, since Irv is gone, I asked if someone from Redstone would come, but we don't have the space right now for troops."

Lena pulled her hair back into a ponytail. "We can talk about the future when they get here." She turned to face Ava. "Is there something you aren't telling me?"

"Nothing too bad. The kids are unhurt, but I don't know what damage the fight did to their spirits. Our neighbors dropped by on their way back. Said you were a warrior and they'd visit soon."

Lena just stared.

"Scott was hurt. Shot, his leg," Ava said. "Deb says it will heal, but he's out of commission for a few months. There's no other news, bad or good."

Lena waited for a heartbeat and then seemed to accept there was nothing more. "Dinner?" she asked, taking Ava's arm. "I'll check on Scott and then come help prepare. And break out the last of the whiskey. We can always make some more."

CHAPTER FORTY-ONE

Lena poured the last of the whiskey into her glass. The house was quiet, and she couldn't sleep. On the porch, the night seemed huge. Stars speckled the sky and the silence was healing. Every muscle and joint hurt. Adrenaline had carried her through killing Cole to sending his men away. Now, she felt every movement of her body. It was painful, but made her feel alive.

Tomorrow she'd start planning again. The farm, the alliances, what to do with the people at the Fort. How to build a stronger community with the smallholders. Maybe a market where people exchanged what they didn't need. Maybe some joint foraging sweeps. There must still be supplies of everything in some big box store out there.

But that was tomorrow. Tonight, she was enjoying the peace. No one looking to her for help or guidance. No fields to work. No mysteries to solve.

She sipped her drink. She'd almost come out without her rifle. The feeling of victory stamping down her common sense. But there it was leaning against the table only an arm's length away.

Footsteps on the gravel. Too soon for the runners to be back. One of Cole's men looking for payback?

Lena reached for the weapon, slowly, not wanting to escalate anything.

It was only one person, limping, head down, a backpack hanging from one shoulder. Two more steps.

A man, road-worn, not battle weary.

Two more steps.

Lena felt the hard-earned peace shred and blow away.

Brian. Her ex-husband.

She stood and pointed the rifle. "Stay where you are."

Brian stopped, raised his head and peered at her. "Lena? It's me."

"I know that. Why are you here?"

"The cities are dying. New Surrey is in the control of gangs."

"You should have believed me," Lena said, knowing it was petty.

"Yes, but I didn't. Now I need you, I need a place to live." He took a step and then halted when Lena raised the rifle. "Can't we put it behind us?"

"Did you bring anyone?" Lena's imagination had a horde of Brian's friends waiting just out of sight. Waiting to take her farm.

"Just me."

This wasn't her decision. Lena reminded herself that she'd been adamant that taking in travelers was a family decision. And Scott needed to know. But she couldn't send Brian on the road at this time of night. "Go to the barn. There's an empty stall. Do you have food?"

"No. I ran out yesterday."

"Go to the barn. I'll bring you something to eat and then we'll see in the morning."

"Not in the house?" Brian asked, surprised. "I thought you'd be happy to see me again. I'm your husband."

Lena saw ownership on his face, not hope over a damaged relationship.

"I'm with someone else. You lost the right to be my husband a year ago. In the barn. Don't disturb the cows, don't use it as a toilet, and don't set anything on fire."

She could see him assessing the risk of simply walking into the house. Wondering if she would shoot to keep him out. Lena didn't know that answer.

"Okay, in the morning."

She watched as Brian entered the barn.

So much for peace and quiet.

WANT MORE?

The final battle for the farm comes in the form of a charismatic preacher. Use the QR code to get your copy of A Question of Sanctuary and join Lena and family in a battle for hearts and minds.

Sneak peek on the next page.

If you enjoyed reading A Fight for Home, please consider helping other readers to find the story by leaving a review.

CHAPTER 1

The farmhouse kitchen was warm and fragrant from the morning's baking. Lena shelled peas with Scott beside her, his presence making her feel safe and grounded. The vegetables would be preserved for the winter. She watched as Mellow and Tik cleaned the dishes. This was her dream all that time ago when she walked out of the city. This peaceful scene.

It had been six months. Scott was still not completely back to normal and without antibiotics, it would be a long time before he was, but Lena no longer worried infections would take him. Now his weakness and determination to ignore it was causing concern. Too much too soon would set him back.

Brian had not yet succeeded in finding a place within the community. Lena didn't see any value coming from him. He wandered off when work was needed and claimed to be thinking about the future when she asked him. He wasn't satisfied and took very few pains to hide the feeling. Lena suspected the others were as tired of his constant nit picking as she was.

But it had also been six months without anyone attacking. The alliance hadn't been tested beyond a bit of skill transferring; the promise of help in an emergency still just that, and it could stay that way forever. She wondered if this was the new reality. If it was, she'd consider every hardship they'd endured to get here worthwhile.

The only blip in the peace was the current encampment of city refugees. The unwelcome visitors would be leaving soon no matter what they planned. The farm was too small to support so many unskilled people. Perhaps Brian would leave with them. His talents proved more useful in larger groups.

"I heard a rumor from the camp," Scott said.

"You've been hanging out with them? Be careful; I'm not sure they know how to keep their camp clean enough. We can't be sure there's no illness lurking." Lena wanted to keep Scott isolated so he wouldn't contract yet another infection. Her logical mind knew it was useless, but death was too easy now. And she didn't know how she'd continue without Scott. The only thing she knew for certain was that she wouldn't return to Brian. Her marriage was dead and buried long ago.

"They're fine." He took the colander of peas to the sink. "A few more come every day. We can't let them camp much longer. Unless you think we can use the labor in the fields?"

"I'm more worried they'll harvest the crops and leave us with nothing," Lena said. "What rumor?"

"A preacher. He's telling everyone we need to repent so God will not send another plague."

"And people believe him?" She wasn't entirely surprised. The plagues happened because people believed nonsense about vaccinations and stopped getting their kids vaccinated. It got so bad, herd immunity was gone and enough people died that civilization collapsed.

"There are a lot of people who don't have what we do," Scott said. "They are scared, and he's charismatic. People will believe anything if someone is promising safety."

"Should we keep the refugees around so we can field an army?"

Lena laughed, but Scott looked serious. "Maybe we should reach out to our allies? Find out what they know?"

Tik looked at Lena from where he was drying dishes. "Isn't that a bit alarmist? There's no problem here. Well, apart from the camp."

He has a point.

"Better too early than too late," she said. "But let's deal with the refugees first. I need to find Brian. He knows how to talk to them."

Mellow wiped her hands and cocked her head toward the back door. "He went out an hour ago. He does that a lot, goes for a walk when there's work to do."

"Maybe we can persuade him to go for a walk with the refugees," Lena said. "It's more his thing anyway. They are looking for a place to start another town, a big one. He'll have a role in managing the whole enterprise."

"Are you trying out your argument on us?" Tik asked. "We would support you telling him to go even without a plan."

"If I thought that would work, I'd do it," Lena said. "Leaving him in the city when we escaped wasn't enough of a hint our marriage was over. He's ignoring anything that doesn't fit in his worldview, including anything that separates us."

"Well, anything except our bedroom door," Scott said.

"I wouldn't count on that lasting," Mellow said. "I see him pacing the hall at night. Like he's building the courage to burst in and demand his marriage bed."

Lena stifled her laugh. It wasn't fair to do this behind Brian's back. She'd find the time to tell him again there is no future for them as a couple. *Maybe he'll listen this time.* "Let's hope he gets over it," she said. "Is everyone out in the fields?"

"The kids are cleaning out the cellar," Scott said. "We'll need more room for food storage this year even with the share going to the alliance. Keith is hunting. Deb is in the camp offering nursing. She said no illness, but there are lots of minor injuries. And there are a few people who exist in a daze. They need counseling, and she's not the right person for that."

"I wonder what skills they brought. Even if they find a town to inhabit, they'll need workers and teachers and doctors," Mellow said.

"It sounds like they're healthy enough to head out. How they build their future isn't our problem." Lena stood and dumped the pea pods into the stock pot.

CHAPTER 2

She saw Brian heading toward the house. Telling him to leave always seemed easy, but when an opportunity came up, she never found the right words. The problem was practical; Brian didn't fit in and wasn't even trying. He had to go. The solution felt a bit too harsh when she tried to simply say the words. No one wanted to send someone out on the road these days. This time she was saved by someone knocking at the door. *Coward.*

"Are you going to help us or not?" A man stood on the porch, arms crossed.

Lena thought she recognized him from New Surrey, but the camp was made up of five or six towns' worth of people. He could be a stranger. It made no difference. No one from the camp listened to her when she tried to explain her side of the problem. They only talked about their needs.

"Good morning, my name is Lena Custordin. It's my land you're camped on."

He unfolded his arms. "Aron Simons."

He gave her no reason to be polite. "Why should I help you? I didn't invite you. I didn't agree you could camp here. As far as I'm concerned, you should go on your way."

He took a step forward as if to enter the house. Lena squared her shoulders and stayed firmly planted in front of the door.

"Your husband told us we could stay," he said.

"You mean Brian. He is not my husband and has no authority. What do you expect me to do with you?"

The question was genuine. Lena had no idea what made the group of refugees think she had any responsibility for their future. They were lucky that she didn't pick up a gun to get them to move.

"You got here and survived. You've been here long enough to know what's going on in the world. We can't simply keep wandering."

It was the first time anyone from the camp had even answered her question.

"What did you do before you left your city?" If she had any doubts left about fleeing that life, Aron's attitude burned them away. In this new world, people needed to be able to look after themselves first. Alliances and assistance came second.

"I was the comptroller. It means I managed the budget."

"I know what a comptroller did." It must be difficult for him now that no one needed his skills. He'd been important in the old world.

"Fine." He took a half step closer and leaned in to intimidate her. "We've been here a week. When are you going to get off your ass and help us out?"

Entitled bastards didn't last long these days. "Go back to the camp and be very happy I'm not the sort to shoot people who annoy me. Pack up and find a place where you are welcome."

"You won't help?" He seemed genuinely shocked.

"I don't know what I can do to help. Go back to the camp and let me talk to my family."

"There are more of us," Aron said.

So, they were down to threats. "Sure. But how many people have you killed to save your property?"

He got the hint. Lena watched him walk back to the camp. They were leaving in the next few days whether or not she could think of a way that didn't require force. And she didn't think it was a good idea to test the alliance by sending them to Crystal. No one needed a pack of people in their community who wouldn't take responsibility for themselves.

Lena returned to the kitchen. No Brian. A good thing because when she saw him, he would find out how happy she was that he'd invited the refugees. And suddenly she didn't feel so bad about telling him he should join the people in the camp.

Scott and Tik leaned together, talking over a map spread out on the table.

"We heard," Scott said looking up at Lena. "You know they aren't going to give up, right?"

"Unreasonable people can be quite stubborn. And I'm not prepared to shoot anyone to make my point. What can we do to help?"

Tik smoothed the map. "It doesn't need to be only helping them." He looked at Scott. "We have an idea."

Why do I feel like this is going to be a hard one to hear?

"Okay," Lena said. She joined them over the map.

"They don't want to start our kind of community," Scott said. "I'm told they think they can get a city working again if they start from scratch."

"You think there's an empty city nearby?" They hadn't explored much, but Crystal and Redstone were barely more than villages. Prosperity was still more like a commune than a town. "And do you agree with them?"

Scott shook his head. "It doesn't matter if we agree they can reboot a city. Just that they believe they can."

"Why don't they just go back to one of the places they deserted?" As much as she wanted this solution, Lena figured it was only postponing the next demand for help.

"They think the future is west of us. They might be right. The

weather gets less extreme the farther west you go. Our idea will
help us too, the whole alliance." Scott pointed to the map. "We
pick a place and take them there. Far enough away they won't
keep visiting for more assistance and their screw ups won't
bounce back on any of us."

Lena looked at the map. A few towns sat not that far from the
farm. Maybe three weeks to a month's travel. The big cities were
too far, but maybe the refugees would settle for a season. "Who
takes them?"

Scott looked at Tik, who looked back down at the map.

"Fine," Scott said. "Me and Tik. You can spare us. We need to
do some exploring. I can manage that. I don't have the stamina to
help with the farm right now. The camp can't travel fast or far in
one go. It will give me a chance to build my endurance."

"We can teach them how to survive as we travel," Tik said.
"We can both hunt well enough."

"It's a plan," Lena said. "You'll be gone for months, maybe
need to winter somewhere. What does Mellow think about the
idea?"

"She'll be fine. And the trip won't be that long if we don't go
too far west. Three months out and we can come back faster. We
can survive a week or so of winter travel."

"You don't need us here," Scott reminded her.

He didn't say she had Brian, but Lena heard the words clearly.
"I will always need you. Both of you."

"Not for work," Scott said. "Brian will have to step up if we
aren't here."

She could manage without Brian too, if he went. The harvest
was in. Keith could hunt for enough food, maybe train Mahir. "I
need to know what the city refugees think about it."

"But we need to explore," Tik said. "If they won't go, we
should still do that."

Lena held up her hand. "I know, but if they won't agree, I need you here to help get rid of them before we're stuck with them forever."

FREE EBOOK

Claim your copy of A Choice to Make when you sign up for my newsletter and get a glimpse of Lena and Brian at the end of the plagues.

ALSO BY PA WILSON

For more books by P A Wilson
Use the QR code below or go to pawilson.ca

ABOUT THE AUTHOR

Perry Wilson is a Canadian author based in Vancouver, BC who has big ideas and an itch to tell stories. Having spent some time on university, a career, and life in general, she returned to writing in 2008 and hasn't looked back since (well, maybe a little, but only while parallel parking).

She is a member of the Vancouver Writers Social Group, The Royal City Literary Arts Society, and The Surrey Writing Workshop. Perry has self-published several novels. She writes the Madeline Journeys, a fantasy series about a high-powered lawyer who finds herself trapped in a magical world, the Quinn Larson Quests, which follows the adventures of a wizard named Quinn who must contend with volatile fae in the heart of Vancouver, and the Charity Deacon Investigations, a mystery thriller series about a private eye who tends to fall into serious trouble with her cases, and The Riverton Romances, a series based in a small town in Oregon, one of her favorite states. Her stand-alone novels are Breaking the Bonds, Closing the Circle, and The Dragon at The Edge of The Map.

For more information
www.pawilson.ca
pawilson@pawilson.ca

ACKNOWLEDGMENTS

People think that the process of writing is solitary. That's not the case for me. I have help from so many people it would be hard to acknowledge everyone, but I'll give it a try.

The support and inspiration I get from my writer's groups is incalculable. The Vancouver Writers Social Group opens my mind to other ways of telling a story. The Royal City Literary Arts Society gives me the opportunity to meet and share with other writers who have more knowledge than I do. The Other 11 Months group is where I learn about getting the words on the page. And my critique group who helps me find the best parts of the story I want to tell. Thanks to all of the members of these great groups.

Last of all, but definitely a huge part of the process, my beta readers. These are the people who love stories and are willing, and more than able, to tell me if my finished story is ready for you, my readers.